Blood Storm
MAGIC

Blood Storm MAGIC

Ella Grey Book Four

JAYNE FAITH

Blood storm magic / a novel by Jayne Faith

Paperback Edition ISBN: 978-1-952156-06-9

Andara Publishers

Edited by: Mary Novak
Proofread by: Tia Silverthorne Bach of Indie Books Gone Wild
Cover by: Deranged Doctor Designs
Interior Design and Formatting by

E.M.
TIPPETTS
BOOK DESIGNS

www.emtippettsbookdesigns.com

Published in the United States of America

Books by
JAYNE FAITH

Ella Grey Series - *urban fantasy*
Stone Cold Magic
Dark Harvest Magic
Demon Born Magic
Blood Storm Magic

Tara Knightley Series - *urban fantasy*
Oath of Blood (prequel)
Edge of Magic
Echo of Bone
Trace of Fate
more to come

Stone Blood Series - *urban fantasy*
Blood of Stone
Stone Blood Legacy
Rise of the Stone Court
Reign of the Stone Queen
War of the Fae Gods
The Oldest Changeling in Faerie

Sapient Salvation Series - *dystopian sci-fi romance*
The Selection
The Awakening
The Divining
The Claiming

My pulse tapped a swift tempo as I watched the arch-demon hone in on me. The giant winged creature circled slowly overhead, but from my Demon Patrol training I knew their behavior well enough to not be fooled by the lazy spiral the hellspawn traced. The interdimensional rip it had emerged from created a backdrop of neon-blue magic. It almost looked like special effects in a movie, but this was no CGI wizardry. It was very real.

I gripped the handle of my razor chain whip tightly, belatedly realizing I should have wrapped it with paper tape or something. A bit of sweat on the palm made it slippery. I was still getting used to the weapon, after a rogue vamp had snapped my old charmed whip.

In my ear, there was a brief pop of static and then a deep voice.

"We've got a clear shot," the Supernatural Special Forces leader said.

"Stand down. Let me take it," I muttered, little white puffs of air punctuating my words. "It's not quite clear of the rip. If you guys start firing, the rip will close again, and you'll spook the hellspawn."

The vertical rip was like a giant cat's pupil framed with bright blue flames. The lower end of the slit almost touched the ground, and the whole thing was nearly three stories tall.

"We've got you if anything goes sideways," the voice said. There was a pause. "Is it wrong that I want to see you pop its head off?"

The corners of my lips twitched in an almost-grin. The voice in my ear belonged to Caleb Montgomery, lead on the team that was backing me up on this job.

"Not wrong at all," I said, my eyes glued to the arch-demon.

The creature's flight was picking up speed, and it was starting to drop in elevation. Specialists had been trying to close the rip for weeks after some high-schoolers had come to this construction site with the bright idea of playing with magic they couldn't control. One of the kids had paid with his life when they'd opened the rip. His buddies were lucky they hadn't died, too. The rip was intermittent—opening and closing at random. There'd been more casualties as specialists tried to seal the thing permanently. Rip-sealing magic was fairly new and only worked on smaller tears. If this rip were any bigger, it wouldn't be a candidate.

My old partner Damien and I had won a contract to accomplish what others hadn't managed—close the rip, kill any lingering demons, and reap the souls of the people who'd died on the site. Damien was gone, having taken Phillip Zarella's offer of mage power. The change had altered Damien in terrible ways and seemed to fuel his life-long obsession with gaining his family's acceptance and approval. The final betrayal was when he took my brother, Evan, who I'd been desperately searching for the past five years and finally rescued from a vampire feeder den. But Evan's ill luck had continued, because he unfortunately held the key to permanently closing the rips.

I still didn't know where Damien was hiding Evan, but I was using my necromancy to deploy minor demons as my spies. I'd commanded several of them and sent them to watch places I thought Damien might go—his hometown back East, a family home in the Hamptons, his loft here in downtown Boise. I'd also been in touch with the madman himself, Zarella, for help, and he was making use of his own resources to try to locate Evan. But so far there was no sign of my brother.

In the meantime, I'd run out of money. That was why I was standing under a giant rip with the aim of beheading an arch-demon.

Before Damien's change, he and I had set up a freelance magical services company, Perfect Circle Supernatural Services. Part of me felt dirty continuing a venture that had any connection to Damien. But my bank account balance remained coldly unsympathetic to my conflicted feelings, and when the company won a couple of the contracts we'd bid on, I couldn't afford to turn down the jobs.

The rip that towered over me had brought not only myself and an SSF Team, but also a trio of mid-Level III crafters who would try to close the tear as soon as I took care of the arch-demon.

This particular rip had been troublesome because each time it opened, dangerous arch-demons flew through. A Special Forces Team would show up to kill the demon before it could possess a human, but the weapon blasts caused the rip to close up again before the magic specialists could permanently sew it closed. And then at some random time, the rip would appear again, releasing more arch-demons and starting the cycle over again.

I'd been hired for this job partly because I was impervious to demon possession. Plus, my time on Demon Patrol had given me ample knowledge of the creatures as well as credentials. I just had to kill the arch-demon in a way that wouldn't cause the rip to disappear before the Level III specialists could snuff it out for good.

I'd recently amped up my magical ability to high III, so far up on the Magical Aptitude Scale I registered at the maximum. Technically, I was more powerful even than the three magic experts here to close the rip, but I didn't have the knowledge or training to close rips. Such an increase in power—any increase at all, actually—was supposed to be impossible. But before Damien had turned mage, he'd figured out how to do it first on himself and then on me. I considered my change a parting gift from my former partner and friend. The irony of it was, when I found him and my brother I would use the full force of my magic to rip Damien apart if I had to.

My pulse kicked up as the arch-demon's wings stilled for a split second. This was it. The creature was going to dive.

I flicked my wrist and my chain whip jumped off the ground. Drawing power and pushing it into my arm, I made the weapon light up with earth, fire, and air magic.

The creature screamed an ear-grating cry as its lizard-like head aimed straight for me. Leathery wings pumped. The smell of sulfur and rot filled my nostrils.

I spun my arm faster, whirling the whip until it blurred. I would only have one chance. If I missed, SSF would fire and the rip would wink out, only to reappear at some other random time. But I had no intention of sending everyone home disappointed.

Directed by my magic, the chain whip curled into a spiral in the air. I pushed more air and earth and then let go, sending the weapon up at the hellspawn. Green filaments of earth trailed from the whip to my palms, and I quickly flicked my arms to send the chain curling around the beast's neck.

When it was nice and snug, I yanked. The arch-demon screeched in fury.

The chain whip responded, its razor-edged links cutting easily into flesh. One more pull, and the chain sliced clear through.

The head broke from the body and dropped to the ground with a heavy-sounding plunk. The rest of the arch-demon remained aloft for a second or two, the wings still pumping by reflex. Then it went limp and crashed to the ground.

The trio of crafters moved in with SSF right behind them to cover in case another demon came through.

I pulled on the earth magic filaments that still connected me to my weapon, and the chain whip snaked along the ground toward me. The crafters and soldiers jumped out of the way.

I stood where I was and watched the Level IIIs work. They swiftly drew magic of the four elements and began to weave it in strands that began to curl together. Within a few seconds, the patterns were too complicated for my eyes to sort out the individual pieces, but the overall shape seemed to be forming into a multi-colored double-helix.

One end of the magic darted to the lower edge of the rip. The magic strands quickly curled upward, like a couple of threads on a giant invisible needle. It literally looked as if the helices were sewing the rip closed.

It seemed to be working. Neon blue rip magic extinguished as soon as the Level III's creation swirled around it. Up and up, the double helix curled the edges of the rip together until it was gone.

The whole thing took maybe five minutes. When it was done, everyone stood in awed silence for a few seconds. Than a few of the higher-ups who'd hung back began to applaud. A few of the SSF Team men and women raised their arms and some victorious shouts went up.

I watched the three Level IIIs shake hands and then reached for water magic, intending to wash the arch-demon ick off my whip before gathering it up. Water magic was my newest trick. It was the most difficult of the four elemental magics to command, and I still sucked at it, but I could draw enough for small tasks.

I closed my eyes briefly to focus. Most beginning magic users devised a little trick to make initial contact with each of the elements. After a lot of practice, experienced crafters didn't need tricks anymore, but it would be a while before I got there. With water, I initiated contact with the element by sending my awareness to the moisture in the environment around me. Easy, if I were near a lake or in a house with plumbing. Not as straightforward outside at a construction site, shivering in the freezing winter air.

"Nice work disposing of the demon, Grey," a deep, warm voice said, interrupting my concentration. My eyes popped open to find Caleb standing there, smiling. "Kind of made Special Forces irrelevant, but I'll try not to let it bruise my ego too badly."

I smiled back. It was hard not to. Caleb had an ever-present twinkle in his green eyes, and his reddish hair was somehow attractively messed up from the helmet he held under one arm. He shifted the helmet so he could reach out his right hand.

I grasped it and gave a modest half-shrug. "It could have taken a bad turn. I'm glad you guys were here."

Caleb was new to the local Supernatural Special Forces division, having just moved to town about a month back. The division had been beefed up after my brother was taken from Rogan's house only hours after we'd rescued Evan from a vampire feeder den. A huge genetically modified demon had been used to facilitate the abduction, and the creature had possessed Rogan. The demon couldn't be exorcised, and it led to Rogan's death. The threat of new and more dangerous hellspawn had brought more firepower to the local Supernatural Forces team.

Caleb and I had crossed paths three times before. Twice on jobs, and once when we'd randomly bumped into each other downtown.

I let go of his hand, and he pointed over his shoulder with his thumb. "Bunch of us are going to the pub, if you'd like to join. We figured since we're all going to be a little amped up for a while, we might as well close the place down."

It was after midnight, and bars closed at two.

"I appreciate the invite, but I've still got work to do on site," I said, keeping purposely vague about the task that remained.

It was tempting to say I'd meet up with them later. I missed the comradery of my Demon Patrol coworkers, and it might have been nice to drink a couple of beers and shoot the shit with the Special Forces people. But I knew by the way Caleb looked at me that he wanted to ask me out, and I just wasn't ready. Rogan had been gone only a month, and his absence was still too fresh.

"Maybe next time?" he asked.

I nodded. "Sure."

The SFF Team was loading up, and the Level III crafters were talking to Detective Barnes, the petite blond lead detective from Supernatural Crimes. She and another detective I'd come to know, Chris Lagatuda, were probably there to wrap up the investigation of the deaths that had occurred.

Since Supernatural Crimes had hired me for this job, both detectives knew that part of my contract involved reaping the souls of the deceased. No one knew exactly why the souls hadn't already departed, but we all assumed it had something to do with the proximity of the intermittent rip.

Since the adrenaline of taking out the arch-demon was starting to wear off, my attention switched to the soft tickle that seemed to emanate from my bones. It was the sense of something waiting out there for me. The souls that wanted to be cut free.

At the thought of reaping, I felt a vague stirring behind my sternum. An angel of death named Xaphan had permanently attached itself to me when I'd temporarily died on the job several months ago. For a while, it looked like the reaper would be the end of me as it chomped away at my soul so it could take over my body. But Phillip Zarella, of all people, had provided the fix that kept Xaphan at bay. I couldn't get rid of the reaper, but that was okay—we'd reached a sort of understanding. I was in charge, and Xaphan was allowed to ride along. My reaper gave me the ability to move between the world of the living and the *in-between*, the realm where reapers roamed and souls of the deceased awaited release to the *beyond*.

I watched the red tail lights of the armored Supernatural Special Forces truck retreat down the dirt road leading away from the construction site. Then I took a deep breath, faced the skeletal structure of the partially finished building, and let my awareness slip into the *in-between*.

The gray mist of the *in-between* drifted low around my legs, puffing and eddying when my movements disturbed it. There was no true night or day in this realm, only weak light and colorless tones.

Not all objects carried over here, and there wasn't a whole lot of rhyme or reason to it. The partially constructed apartment development looked essentially the same in the *in-between* as it did in the realm of the living, but I noticed that the young trees the landscapers had planted before winter set in didn't exist here.

Neither Barnes nor Lagatuda, who'd moved several yards away to stand near their Supernatural Crimes cruiser, were visible in limbo land either. The living never were.

I let my reaper come forth, giving in to the sense that drew us toward the still-tethered souls. One was a teenager, one of the kids who'd been fooling around with magic and accidentally opened the rip. The human part of me felt sadness that someone so young had lost his life, but the reaper felt no emotion, only single-minded focus.

That was the soul I was drawn to first. The boy had lost his life near the front left corner of the unfinished building. His soul appeared as a vacant-eyed, wispy specter that floated several feet above the ground, held like a helium balloon by a gossamer strand extending from one foot down to the spot where he'd died.

As if by reflex, my right hand lifted with a preternaturally sudden movement. In the skeletal fingers, a short knife appeared.

The blade's metal appeared dull in the faint, ethereal light of the *in-between*, but the edge was diamond-sharp.

The filament holding the boy's soul in this realm pulled at me, almost hypnotizing me. When I drew near, the soul seemed to wake up, jerking and straining at the cord that held it.

With a movement so swift it had to be the reaper controlling it, the knife flicked out and severed the cord. The soul winked out, but not before a look of serenity crossed the boy's face.

I turned and stalked to the next soul, this one belonging to an adult who'd perished on the second floor. A swing of the blade, and another soul freed. The third victim had died on the top floor, a witch who'd reportedly come to try to collect some of the neon-blue magic licking from the rip. It was illegal, and for good reason—the properties of rip magic weren't well-understood, and it was obviously extremely dangerous to get that close to an interdimensional tear.

My reaper's blade severed the gossamer strand, and the woman's soul departed.

The knife disappeared from my hand, and I turned to look out at the mist-shrouded view. Something different called to me since the pull of the unreaped souls was gone. This realm had its own ley lines, veins of powerful magic that ran through the ground, and the sense of it pulsed through my veins. When I'd first touched the silver ley line magic of the *in-between*, it had rushed into me in a torrent I couldn't control, and it had nearly killed me. I could channel it in manageable amounts, but doing so came at a price. Humans weren't supposed to be able to use it, and every time I did, it brought searing pain and gave my brain a beating, increasing my risk of sudden death. I hadn't touched the silver magic in many days, but I assumed I'd have to call upon it when I located my brother.

I went back to the first floor and then released my connection with the *in-between*, passing back into the land of the living and regaining my normal mortal form.

Barnes and Lagatuda were still waiting, but they weren't the only ones left on site. I recognized Johnny Beemer's Mustang parked next to the cruiser.

Ugh. Running into an ex, always a great way to end the night.

With a stifled sigh, I trudged away from the construction as he stepped out and slammed the driver door closed. I thought his gaze flicked my way, but he was too distant and it was too dark for me to read his expression.

By the time I'd joined the detectives, Johnny had retrieved a black case from the trunk of his car. I knew it contained one of his gadgets. Though not a magic user himself, he had a slew of specialized equipment that could detect various supernatural phenomena. He was in high demand as a freelancer, and I supposed it was only a matter of time before we ran into each other on a job.

Barnes stepped forward. "Everything go okay?" she asked.

I nodded. "Three souls departed. The kid, a man, and a woman."

She turned her head, her blond ponytail swinging over her shoulder, to watch Johnny approach. "We'll just verify that the site is clear, and then you can go."

Awesome, she'd called in my ex-boyfriend to check my work. I shoved my fists deep into my coat pockets. I knew his presence wasn't anything personal, but it was still annoying. Johnny and I hadn't split on friendly terms.

"Hi, Ella," Johnny said, his voice low and tone chilly. His gaze skipped to me and then beyond to the construction site.

"Hello, Johnny." I managed to sound friendly, I thought, but his face remained hard.

He wasn't really a bad guy. We just kind of sucked as a couple.

He set his case on the ground, opened it, and removed a souped-up tablet that had extra little doohickies and wires attached it. Already focused on his task, he moved off toward the building.

I turned to the detectives, my thoughts already jumping back to my meager bank balance. "I don't suppose you know of any more jobs I might be suited for, off the top of your head?"

Lagatuda, a tall man dressed in one of his many nearly identical suits, gave me a faint smile of sympathy. He'd taken an interest in my best friend Deb, who was pregnant, nearly divorced, and living with me in my tiny apartment, and knew that she and I were a bit financially challenged at the moment.

"You know I don't have the authority to take you under contract," Barnes said. "You have to go through the formal application process."

I resisted the temptation to roll my eyes. Did she always have to be such a hard ass? It was so incongruent with her appearance—she looked like a perky little former high school cheerleading captain—but maybe that was part of why she felt she had to act the way she did.

"I do know that," I said patiently. "I was just wondering if you might have heard of anything coming through."

"Let's get the paperwork on this one finished, and then we'll see," she said.

She turned her attention to Johnny, and Lagatuda shot me a wide-eyed look of exasperation over her head. I pulled in my lips and bit down to keep from snorting a laugh. Maybe he was just taking my side because he had a crush on Deb, but either way, he was a lot easier to deal with than Barnes and probably my greatest ally at SC.

While we waited for Johnny, I tuned into my necro senses. I'd become much more skilled at commanding minor demons, the bat-like creatures that occasionally spilled through rips. My necromancy gave me the ability to penetrate their minds, control them, and see through their eyes. Rogan had been able to control multiple arch-demons at once, but I didn't yet have the skill to penetrate the mind of even one of them. Seemed to be the story of my life lately: plenty of abilities, but not enough skill or experience to take full advantage of them.

After Damien had stolen Evan, I'd sent minor demons out to scour the city but had found no trace of my former partner or my brother. Setting up minor demons as lookouts was like expecting to identify a terrorist by monitoring only a handful of random security cameras, because I'd learned when Damien disappeared with Evan that the newly made mage had the ability to teleport. He literally could be anywhere at any time. But I'd had to do *something*, even if it was about as useful as screaming into the wind.

My fingers twitched with impatience as I checked in with each of my demon minions. If any of them had spotted Damien, I would have known, but I couldn't help rotating my awareness around to each creature. It'd almost become a nervous tic.

I knew it was unlikely I'd find my brother on my own. That was why I'd had to turn to Phillip Zarella, the powerful but psychotic necromancer who'd been in hiding ever since he'd faked his own death. Zarella had his own reasons for wanting to get Evan back, but I'd worry about that once we'd recovered my brother.

Johnny finished his scan of the site and came back to where we stood.

He gave me an approving nod. "The site is clear of unreaped souls," he said. "No trace of active rip activity anymore, either."

"Fabulous," Barnes said. "We'll wrap this up on our end."

"When can I expect payment?" I asked.

She shot me an irritated look. "What, do you think I'm in charge of accounting, too?"

I raised my palms, giving her an innocent, wide-eyed look. "Just asking."

"Within ten business days," Lagatuda supplied, taking pity on me.

"Thank you." I gave him a pointedly sweet smile and then turned my exaggerated pleasantness onto Barnes. "It was a pleasure doing business with you."

I wheeled around and walked swiftly toward my truck, suddenly feeling drained. It sapped a lot of energy to have to suck up to someone like Barnes.

In my pickup, I passed a hand over my tired eyes and then started the engine. Lulled by the heat blasting through the vents once the engine was finally warm, I went on autopilot as I drove toward home. It was late, and I wanted my bed.

A few blocks from my apartment, my phone began vibrating and chirping insistently on the passenger seat. I picked it up, wondering who could be contacting me at that hour. When I saw the name on the message, my fatigue fled.

It was the code name Phillip Zarella used. That meant he had news about Damien.

Zarella contacted me using burner phones, so the number was never the same. But the name was one he'd picked, an unusual one so that I'd know it was him.

Meet me in your back yard when you arrive at home.
–Alois

A shiver skittered up my spine. Zarella himself wouldn't be waiting at my apartment. It would be one of the zombies he commanded. As a powerful and practiced necromancer, he could drive zombie minds and use them as his eyes, ears, and voice. This wouldn't be the first time I'd carried on a conversation with him as he used one of his zombies as a ventriloquist dummy, but it wasn't something I'd ever be totally easy with.

I steered through the streets of Boise's North End, a neighborhood of sought-after pristine old homes, houses converted to businesses or apartments like my building, and a few ramshackle places that hadn't been kept up. As expected, the windows of my apartment were dark. It was way past Deb's bedtime—hell, it was past my bedtime—so I parked at the curb, killed the engine, and went around to the back so I wouldn't disturb her.

When I opened the gate, I spotted a too-still figure sitting in one of my deck chairs. Trying not to cringe, I closed the latch and approached the zombie. The area was saturated with the burnt sage smell of the strong magic that kept the rot at bay and covered the smell of a body that was animated, but not exactly alive anymore. Through the scent of the magic, there was an undertone of something wild and musky-smelling that I tried my best to ignore.

I swallowed hard as the figure stood in an almost-natural movement. Zarella had sent this zombie before—a lanky olive-skinned man. I pulled my jacket tighter around me.

The zombie's mouth opened. "Ella, so good to see you," he intoned. It was Zarella speaking through the creature's throat.

The master necromancer was skilled, the movements of the jaw and mouth nearly smooth enough to be mistaken for a live human.

"Alois," I said. I stood a few feet off, farther away than was socially acceptable in normal situations. But I wasn't concerned with offending Zarella, and the zombie sure as hell didn't care. "You have news?"

There was faint scratching at the back door, and Loki, my hellhound-labradoodle let out a soft whine. I silently willed him to stay quiet. The last thing I needed was to alert my neighbors that there was a zombie in the yard. Victims of the NECR2 virus, which caused zombieism, were supposed to be euthanized. The creature I was talking to wasn't supposed to be roaming around.

"I do. I have located Damien."

My heart skipped a beat. "What about Evan?"

"He hasn't been sighted, but I assume he is nearby."

"Where's Damien?"

The zombie paused. "There is the matter of—"

"What, payment?" I cut in. "You know I have no money."

I hadn't expected Zarella to give his aid for free, but I didn't have much to offer.

"No, not money," the zombie said. "I want your promise of help, when the time comes."

I frowned. "Help with what?"

It wasn't going to be good. It couldn't. Zarella was a psychopath who was supposed to be dead. He'd been imprisoned for a long list of atrocities and then faked his own death during a jailbreak. My uncle, mogul Jacob Gregori who had his own rap sheet of crimes against humanity, had been secretly providing Zarella asylum on the nearly impenetrable campus of Gregori Industries.

"I'll need some assistance to permanently secure my freedom out here in the wild. But don't worry, your task will be simple," the zombie said. "There will be no blowback on you, rest assured."

I narrowed my eyes. "I'm not going to be involved in hurting anyone."

"No harm will come to anyone who doesn't deserve it."

"That's not good enough," I said, shaking my head.

"What choice do you have, Ella? Would you refuse me and take the chance of losing your dear brother?"

My mouth pinched, and my nostrils flared.

"I hold you in the palm of my hand," the zombie said. "We both know that. You'd best accept it."

I ground my teeth. "No killing, mutilating, or otherwise physically harming anyone. And nothing that will land me in prison."

"No, I would not ask you to do any of those things. You're not a monster. I don't desire to turn you into one. Nor do I desire to see you incarcerated."

Gee, what a kind consideration coming from a man whose experiments had been on par with Nazi "research."

"Fine," I said. "I'll do your required task when the time comes. Now, where's Damien?"

"He's in San Francisco."

"Can you be more specific?" I snapped, my patience wearing thin.

"There's no point in you going there," the zombie said. "He's turned his quarters into a fortress. You'll never get in."

My arms clamped hard against my sides.

"You don't get to tell me what I can and can't do, *Alois*," I spat out. "The only thing I care about is my brother. I'm not going to let Damien offer him up as a sacrifice."

I didn't have confirmation that was what Damien planned, but there was no other reason for him to take Evan. Everyone wanted my brother—Zarella and his chaos-loving cronies, my uncle, and the Order of Mages. Zarella wanted to prevent anyone else using Evan to close the giant rips that still threatened us, Jacob wanted to sacrifice Evan to finally atone for the sin of opening the rips in the first place, and the mages probably wanted to do the same as Jacob, except as a powerplay rather than atonement.

Damien's life-long obsession with increasing his magical ability to mage level and finally gaining the approval of his powerful mage family made it obvious: he was going to give my brother to the Steins and the Order so Damien could have the acceptance he'd longed for since birth.

It was Zarella's fault that I was in this situation in the first place. He'd offered Damien the chance to do the impossible—go from a Level III to a mage—in return for retrieving a small box. I'd found the empty box at Damien's apartment but still didn't know what it had contained. Zarella had warned us that the transition to mage would turn Damien into a different person, stripping him of his humanity. But my former partner had taken the deal anyway. And once he became a mage, he'd stolen my brother.

Yet there I stood, making another deal with the psycho and needing his help. It all made my brain hurt and made me long for the old days when all I had to worry about was walking my beat on Demon Patrol.

"I only meant that you can't go in alone," the zombie said. "You need backup."

I crossed my arms. "I assume you have an idea about who that backup should be."

The zombie nodded. "I have some like-minded friends who do not want to see the Order of Mages murder your brother."

"You mean they don't want the rips closed."

Zarella believed that the rips—and whatever hellspawn and other catastrophes they brought—should remain as they were. Welcomed, even. He wanted darkness to surge into the world. He desired chaos. Rogan had warned me that there were others like Zarella in the Society of the Underworld.

"They don't want the Order of Mages taking over the world," the zombie countered.

I didn't give a crap about the mages and their hunger for more power. I just didn't want my brother to be a pawn in anyone's scheme. Evan had been a troubled kid and an addict teenager, and at nearly twenty years old, he'd yet to have the opportunity at anything resembling a normal life.

I sighed as my former fatigue started creeping back. "Whatever. But I want a shot a Damien."

"You're no killer."

I crossed my arms and looked off to the side. He was right.

"What's next, then?" I asked.

"Your brother is safe for now, so just hold tight until I can mobilize the others."

"Fine," I said, and turned to go inside.

"A warning, Ella," he called as I unlocked the door.

I looked over my shoulder.

"If you spook Damien and he disappears again, you'll blow our chance."

I went inside and locked the door behind me. Loki jumped at me, pushing his front paws against my chest and lapping at my face with his big, smelly tongue.

"Down, boy," I said with a small laugh, fending him off with my hands.

He dropped to the floor and turned sideways so he could lean into me. I scratched behind his ears and then went to dump a scoop of dog food into his bowl.

While he chomped his kibble, I leaned against the counter, too tired to do much of anything but also too tired to get ready for bed.

Closing my eyes, I reached out with my necro senses and released the minor demons I had stationed around a few places back East where I thought Damien might go. Then I pulled my awareness to the immediate vicinity and located half a dozen of the bat-like creatures lurking within a few blocks. Finding the active little points of energy that represented their minds, I pushed my power. It was like sticking your finger into a rotted orange, and I cringed every time. But within a few seconds, I'd penetrated the minds of the minor demons and sent them off to San Francisco. It would take them time to get there, and it was probably another pointless exercise, but at least I knew the general area where Damien was hiding out.

And despite Zarella's warning not to interfere until he had his people ready, I wasn't going to just sit around and wait. I needed to be ready to go to San Francisco at a moment's notice.

I went to the living room and fell onto the sofa, not bothering to pull out the foldout. With one arm behind my head and Loki stretched out along my legs, I took out my phone and started doing some research on the San Francisco Bay Area.

I woke with a start early the next morning with my phone vibrating on my chest. I'd been dreaming of my brother, and the dream was like an echo of the visions I used to have of him before I'd located him in the vampire feeder den. But it wasn't a vision. My reaper never gave those to me anymore. It was just a plain old dream.

Sitting up and pushing my hair back from my face, I stretched and yawned so wide my jaw cracked. Deb walked out of the bathroom in her terry robe and with a towel turbaned around her head just in time to see my mouth gaping open.

Her brows rose. "Late night?" she asked, tightening the robe's tie above the swell of her belly. She was past the halfway mark in her pregnancy.

I nodded and croaked something in the affirmative. I blinked hard, trying to clear the brain haze of sleep and strange dreams.

Clearing my throat, I tried again. "I took care of the arch-demon, and the magical specialists closed the rip," I said.

"Nice, that must have been something to see." She pulled the towel from her head and began finger-combing her damp strawberry blond hair. "Maybe there's hope for permanently closing all the rips."

I pushed off the edge of the sofa and stood. "Eh, the magic is apparently not developed enough to handle bigger ones. Experts are saying the new techniques can't be scaled up. The Boise Rip and the Manhattan Rip aren't going anywhere anytime soon."

Some of the interdimensional tears were permanent, the original and biggest of them being located in New York.

"Well, one can hope," she said in her typical sunny-minded fashion.

Yeah, except the best chance for ending the rips permanently seemed to require murdering my brother. At least, that was what Jacob Gregori and the Order of Mages claimed. Apparently, Evan possessed the precise type of magic that made him the one and only ideal conduit for channeling the power that would seal the rips. Jacob had claimed my parents had me for this aim, but I hadn't come out quite right for the job. Evan had.

I started toward the kitchen to get a pot of coffee started but paused in the arched doorway.

"Lagatuda was there," I said, watching her for a reaction.

Her fingers paused in her hair for a split-second. "Was he?" she asked, her disinterest a bit too forced for me to believe it.

"Aw, c'mon, I know the two of you have been talking," I said teasingly.

Her mouth dropped open, and she gave me an affronted look. "Have you been spying on me?"

I laughed. "No, I can tell by the look you get on your face whenever he texts you."

The living room was too dark to see for sure, but I would have bet she was blushing.

"I'm still technically married, Ella," she mumbled. By the way she said it, it seemed she was trying to remind herself rather than me. "I shouldn't have contacted him at all when he gave you his card."

"Yeah, but you're not gonna be married for much longer," I said. I leaned against the doorway, watching as she folded the towel that had been wrapped around her head. "It's okay, you know. You and Keith are done. There's nothing wrong with talking to another man. There's nothing wrong with being *interested* in another man. You deserve happiness. Besides, it's not like you've been out on a date with the guy. A little harmless texting is okay."

"I don't know why a man like Chris would be interested in someone like me, anyway." A little smile played across her lips, at odds with her words. "Pregnant, broke, and not quite divorced."

"Um, because you're amazing," I said, turning into the kitchen. If I didn't get some caffeine in my system very soon, I was going to fall over. "Your circumstances don't change that basic fact. If Lagatuda sees that, more power to him. I say enjoy it."

"What do you think of him, really?" she called from the bathroom.

I hesitated. No one was good enough for Deb, in my not-at-all-humble opinion, but I supposed I had to be at least a little bit realistic about the fact that she wasn't the type to stay single. After a childhood spent in foster care, she craved close bonds and had always dreamed of having a large family.

"Honestly . . . I guess you could do worse," I said grudgingly. "I suppose he can't be a complete idiot if he likes you so much. And unlike your soon-to-be-ex, he has a real big-boy career with a decent paycheck. He gets points for that."

Deb's husband had constantly chased the lure of an easy fortune, blowing all their money on get-rich-quick schemes that never panned out. He'd even taken her beloved Honda that she'd driven since we first met in high school and sold it. So, in terms of financial responsibility, just about any man was a big step up from the pyramid scheme addict she'd married.

"I've never heard you speak so glowingly of a man," she said with a giggle. "Seriously, that's like a ticker tape parade, coming from you. High school marching bands, Rockettes, washed-up pop stars on floats, big balloon cartoon characters, the whole works."

"I'll still murder him in his sleep if he does anything to hurt you," I growled.

She laughed again. "Aw, don't you go and get all mushy on me. But it really doesn't matter. I'm being dead serious when I say Chris and I are just friends, and that's the way it's going to stay. I'm having a baby in a few months. I don't have time for dating."

"Sure, sure," I said lightly. I knew she felt conflicted about even some innocent texting with Chris when she wasn't divorced yet, but her growing feelings for Chris were clear.

"So, you thinking about getting back on the dating horse?" Deb asked.

The image of Caleb Montgomery, with his sparkly green eyes and one-dimpled grin, sprang to my mind.

"Nah," I said.

"You hesitated."

"No, I didn't."

"Did too. Who is it?"

"Nobody," I said. "I'm not ready for that."

She let it go, and I got a pot of coffee going, opened the back door so Loki could bound out into the yard, and then poured myself a cup before the machine had quite finished its brewing cycle. Scalding my tongue, I drank half the mug before my hellhound-doodle scratched to come back in only a minute later. He looked up at me expectantly. The gargoyle that liked to roost my tiny yard was absent, so there was nothing fun for Loki to antagonize out there.

"Dude, you don't expect me to play fetch, do you? We both know you're not really that kind of dog."

He wagged his tail and gave me a doggy smile, tiny licks of hellfire dancing in his dark pupils, and I cracked a grin and ruffled the top of his shaggy head.

Once the caffeine started to kick in, my thoughts returned to Damien and San Francisco. He'd never mentioned any friends or other connections to that area, but that didn't necessarily mean anything. In the past couple of months, I'd realized I didn't know him nearly as well as I'd assumed.

Part of me was itching to take off and start searching. But I couldn't just go to the Bay Area and wander around with my minor demons, hoping to catch a glimpse of him or Evan. Damien wasn't stupid.

Instead of my usual impulsive reaction, I needed to try to glean some info first. And I planned to start with Damien's loft. I'd recently checked to see whether he'd kept his lease, and as far as I could tell, no one new had moved in. He'd left town in a hurry, using his mage magic to teleport right out of Lynnette Leblanc's house with Evan. I hoped Damien had been in too big a rush to take anything from his loft because I planned to tear the place apart looking for any hint of where I might find him.

Then I'd head for San Francisco. I didn't have mage magic, but Rogan had taught me how to use the *in-between* to instantly move long distances. I wouldn't even have to book a plane ticket.

"Ella?" Deb appeared in the kitchen doorway. "Anybody home?"

"Sorry, what?" I'd gotten more absorbed in my thoughts than I'd realized.

"The coven meeting tonight. I'll swing by and get you after work, okay?"

"Sure," I said, carefully neutral.

Deb and I belonged to a coven led by Lynnette Leblanc, a powerful and manipulative witch. I'd never intended to end up in such a group, but she'd used her verbal magic on me when I needed a favor from her, and I'd unwittingly found myself roped in. Deb had been ecstatic about my membership—she had been trying to get me to join for ages—but in the months I'd been part of the coven, I'd discovered just how dangerous Lynnette was. I wanted Deb out, and of course I wanted to leave as well, but for the moment we were both bound to the group.

Things had taken an interesting turn in the past few weeks, though. Lynnette had gotten herself in trouble with a dragon oracle and had to give up one of her most prized magical skills as punishment: her exorcism talent. Around the same time, my own magical ability had been amped up by a spell Damien created before he turned mage, and I'd become far more powerful than she was, in terms of pure magical aptitude. I wasn't yet very skilled with my newfound power, but the dynamic between me and Lynnette had shifted. She seemed torn between resenting my magical strength and an itching curiosity about the spell behind the phenomenon, no doubt so she could try to use it on herself. Because there was really only one thing Lynnette Leblanc cared about, and that was power.

In her quest for power, Lynnette had secretly started harvesting magic from around small rips that she was opening. She'd attracted the wrong kind of attention for it, which ended up getting one of the witches in her coven killed. The tragedy was actually what had opened a spot in her coven that I ended up taking.

It wasn't the only reckless thing Lynnette had done, but somehow she never seemed to get caught. In fact, losing her exorcism magic when she crossed the dragon oracle was the first time she'd had to pay for her actions.

I hoped it was only the beginning of her downfall, which couldn't come fast enough for my liking.

In the meantime, I was keeping a close eye on Lynnette and trying to chip away at Deb's faith in the coven leader.

It was slow going, though. Deb was often too trusting by nature, Lynnette was a charismatic leader, and the tight-knit coven fulfilled a large part of Deb's longing for family.

As soon as Deb left for work in my pickup, I went to the kitchen, plugged the drain, and filled the sink with about two inches of water. Then I closed my eyes and let go of the realm of the living, turning to the presence of the reaper inside me and allowing us to reach for the *in-between*. Deb was aware of my ability to use the *in-between* to teleport, but I never did it in front of her. This was the trick Rogan had taught me. And that was probably why I always did it alone. He'd shown me how once he'd returned to his reaper form, only hours after he'd been possessed by a new form of hellspawn and then died for it, finally releasing him back to his home in the *in-between*. It had been the last time I'd seen him in any form, and so somehow the thing he'd shown me felt private, almost sacred.

Sensing an adventure, Loki popped into limbo land a second later, the mist of the gray place billowing away from him as he shook his spectral hellhound form and then looked up at me expectantly.

Again, I pulled my attention inward, this time to my mind's eye. I pictured the interior of Damien's loft, and specifically the large bowl of water I'd left on the counter last time I'd been there.

There were a couple of catches. You had to know your destination well enough to picture it in detail, and there had to be water there. Water was the thing that connected the two locations. Beyond that, I didn't have a clue how it worked.

Holding Damien's kitchen in my mind's eye, I reached into the sink of water with my bony reaper's hand and trailed my fingers across the surface. It shimmered and then clarified. And then I was there, standing with Loki in the *in-between* version of an expensive downtown Boise loft.

I changed my focus to the human-Ella part of me, and the *in-between* dissolved away, sharpening into the colors and forms of the living realm.

With a slight shiver, I looked around at the abandoned loft where Damien and I had spent hours planning out our new business venture, sparring on his practice mats with various weapons, and just shooting the shit. But that was the past. That Damien was gone.

"Okay, boy," I said to Loki. "Let's see what we can dig up."

I didn't know whether Damien had returned to his loft in the time since he'd disappeared from Lynnette's guest room with my brother. I'd come to Damien's place right after, hoping to catch him, but with his mage power he could transport himself anywhere in an instant, and of course he hadn't been there.

Damien's laptop was gone, but he'd left the one he'd bought for me—a business expense, he said, and because he didn't want to share his. I almost smiled, thinking of the time we'd spent hunched over the kitchen island scouring the supernatural contract job listings.

I didn't really want anything from Damien, but I'd finally caved and taken the laptop when I realized I did need it for work. Getting it out of Damien's loft had required an interesting little dance between realms and some running around. I'd unlocked the loft's front door, gone down to the lobby and hidden the laptop behind a planter, then hurried back to the loft to re-lock the door and use the *in-between* to transport myself to a nearby location where there was a small fountain. From there I'd walked back to the lobby to retrieve the laptop. All so I could get in and out and keep the loft's door locked.

Yeah, my life was really fricking weird these days.

I went to the modern, minimal desk that was set up against one of the large windows. It had a slim center drawer that held a few pens, a package of business envelopes, and a pad of sticky notes. The only other drawer, large enough to accommodate file folders, contained an unopened package of printer paper and a small notebook.

My pulse jumped when I picked up the notebook, but flipping through it revealed it hadn't been used. I tossed it back.

Did I really expect Damien to have left me easy clues? He wasn't sloppy, and he wasn't stupid. But there was a part of me that still held onto the idea that in his transition to mage some things might have slipped his mind. Zarella had warned me that if Damien took the offer of mage power, he wouldn't be the same person afterward. The old Damien was neat and careful. But maybe the new Damien wasn't quite as meticulous.

I went to the kitchen and systematically opened every drawer and cabinet but didn't find anything interesting. I rummaged through the freezer, which contained a bag of mixed vegetables, half a dozen frozen dinners, an open box of ice cream bars, and a half gallon of mint chocolate chip. The fridge was empty except for condiment containers.

There wasn't a lot in the way of décor, but I peeked behind everything on the walls, moved all the furniture, and rifled through cushions. Using the tip of my pocket knife, I pried up all the vents to see if he'd hidden anything in the ducts.

As I moved around the main living space, Loki followed me, peering at the things I touched and sniffing everything that was in the reach of his nose. But after a while he lost interest and jumped up onto the sofa.

I skipped the guest bath, as there were no cabinets. Last, I went into the master suite.

The bed was neatly made, but the hamper was overflowing. I started with the nightstand and went through the entire room but didn't come across anything significant. Ditto for the bathroom.

I flipped on the light in the walk-in closet and went straight for the stuff on the shelf over the clothes rods. First, a set of three suitcases, all empty. Next, a plastic tub, one of the big ones people use to store Christmas decorations or craft supplies.

It was heavy, and I had the sense even before I opened it that if there was anything in the damn apartment that would help me, it would be in there.

I lifted the lid, and on top a family portrait stared back at me. It was a framed photograph, eight by ten, displaying a man, woman, and three tow-headed children ranging in age from about six to ten years. I knew the adults—I'd seen them at Gregori Industries. They'd stood with Jacob and Damien and peered at me through glass as if I were a monkey at the zoo. They were Damien's parents, mages of the legendary Stein family. The youngest child in the picture had to be Damien—even at that age his wide blue eyes, straight brow, and high cheekbones betrayed how handsome he would be. The other boy and girl were obviously his siblings, but I realized he'd never even mentioned their names.

One conversation came flooding back as I held the picture frame. Damien had told me that his family used to have a portrait like this taken every year, but they did two versions. One with the full family. The other that excluded Damien, because he was the only one of the Steins who wasn't a mage.

A pang gripped the center of my chest as I remembered his face as he'd told me the story. It wasn't that he'd been sad or angry that had left such an impression on me, but that he'd seemed so matter-of-fact. He described something that was horrible to me but to him was simply normal. He'd been treated as a second-class citizen in his own family, and that was just his reality from the day he was born. It was the thing that had driven most of his decisions as an adult, his obsessive quest to increase his own magical aptitude. His longing for acceptance was what had driven him to take Evan. It was what had brought me to be where I was at that very moment, digging through his private things while Damien held my brother captive somewhere in San Francisco.

I set the photo aside and began to dig through the box in earnest. There were framed diplomas and more family portraits, which weren't any help in my quest. I piled them next to me. Then I got into more random items. A mug with a picture of the Statue of Liberty. A seven-year-old playbill from a theater in Chicago. A plastic food storage box labeled "photos" with several memory sticks in it. A well-thumbed copy of Heinlein's *Stranger in a Strange Land*. A few souvenir art books from famous museums in Europe. More small trinkets from various locations. A shoebox stuffed with vintage baseball cards from the 80s and 90s. A stack of letters rubber-banded together. I checked the postmarks, but none were from California, and I didn't have the patience to read through all of them.

I paused to turn each item in my hands, realizing again how little Damien had spoken of his past.

Toward the bottom of the tub, I uncovered a loose stack of pictures. The top one was of Damien a few years younger than he was now, smiling and leaning into a good-looking guy with medium-dark skin, fashionably short stubble, and deep brown eyes. A piece of the San Francisco Bay Area's Golden Gate Bridge took up much of the background.

My interest pinged.

There were more photos taken on the same day, judging by the same clothes they wore. Most of the pics were close-cropped selfies. In one, the dark-haired guy was planting a kiss on Damien's cheek. My former partner's eyes sparkled, and his white teeth gleamed in a broad smile. I wasn't sure I'd ever seen him display that kind of beaming happiness.

I shuffled through the photos a second time and flipped them over to see if he'd written anything on them, but there were no notes on the backs. I made a mental note to look through any old social media posts I could find to see if Damien might have mentioned this trip to San Francisco, or if I could discover anything about the man in the photos.

There weren't any other personal photos in the box. Damien kept only the old family portraits and these pictures even though he wasn't with the other guy in them anymore.

The rest of the box held a stack of notebooks like the one he'd carried around in a backpack all the time, and these ones appeared to hold similar notes about magic. I put them next to the memory sticks for later perusal.

From the bottom of the empty box I plucked a pen. At first, I thought it had probably ended up in there on accident because it looked like an ordinary ballpoint pen, and the casing had a hairline crack. But when I rotated it, I realized it had words printed on it.

The Fairmont Heritage Hotel on Ghirardelli Square. Damien and his ex must have stayed there during their trip. It would be a familiar place for Damien.

I didn't know the hotel, but I'd heard of the landmark. It was right in the heart of San Francisco.

My mouth went dry. I pulled out my phone and punched in the address. When it came up in a maps app, I tapped the map, changed to street view, and then moved around the area. I needed water. A pond or a fountain would do, but I didn't see anything immediately near the hotel. But the famous Pier 45 and Fisherman's Wharf were only a few blocks away from the square. I tapped the map marker for the pier and then did an image search. I had to be able to picture my destination in detail to use the trick of the *in-between*. Zooming in, I examined the pictures near the water. There was a huge dock where the retired Navy vessel USS Pampanito served as a museum and memorial. I enlarged the images even more and examined them, taking in the detail. Assuming the photos weren't too outdated, I should have enough to visualize where I wanted to go.

I paused, staring off into space. Zarella had threatened me, telling me not to interfere. But I thought I could turn Damien. If he was there with his ex, it meant he hadn't severed all connections with his former life. It was a sentimental move to hide out in a place where the two of them had stayed together. I just needed to remind Damien he didn't need to do something terrible to prove himself.

Together, Damien and I could protect Evan. Damien knew more than anyone else in the world about doing impossible things with magic. He could find a way to close the rips, to appease the mages and Jacob, without killing my brother. Damien could be the savior of the modern era.

Tucking my phone away, I grabbed one of the pics of Damien and his ex. I left the rest of the memorabilia of Damien's life scattered on his closet floor and went to the kitchen sink, where I turned my awareness inward to my reaper. Loki, who'd been lounging on the expensive faux-leather sofa, jumped to the floor and trotted over. The realm of the living faded to the grays of the *in-between*, and Loki appeared beside me. I trailed my fingers in the water, pictured the dock, and waited for the shimmer and shift.

And then I was there standing on the wide dock that was so large its movement on a silent sea was almost imperceptible. A gray-toned form of a huge old ship loomed next to the dock. Not wanting to pop into the realm of the living and startle tourists, I stayed in limbo land and headed inland toward Ghirardelli Square.

Loki loped along beside me, seemingly reinvigorated now that we were moving. We ran down the ghost town sidewalks, avoiding the phantom-like cars with their drivers who were only visible in the living realm.

Pausing in an alley near the square, I released my connection to the *in-between* and the world around me gained color, noise, and movement. Once again in the realm of the living, Loki and I set off at a slower pace. My big dog, trotting beside me unleashed, drew some looks. The hellhound-doodle was scary-big at first glance, but I knew he would behave. As long as no one looked too closely at the faint red glow in his eyes, we shouldn't run into any trouble. Hellhounds had come through the Manhattan Rip along with demons, and the otherworldly dogs weren't allowed to roam free. Actually, as far as most people knew, they'd all been rounded up and killed.

The Fairmont Heritage Hotel came into view and I slowed, suddenly unsure of my next move. Damien had no doubt warded the hotel, if he was indeed in there, but I didn't have to worry about that. Ever since the reaper had hitched a ride on my soul, I could walk through wards without setting them off.

But Damien likely wouldn't have stopped at wards. He probably had other precautions in place.

I stopped near the corner of a business high-rise and leaned against the building, trying to look casual. Loki came and sat beside me, casting me questioning looks as if to ask why we'd paused. Tuning into my necro senses, I reached out with my awareness, searching for the active little areas of demonic energy that told me where nearby minor demons were lurking.

The small, bat-like creatures were like rats—you could try to get rid of them, but they found places to hide, and more leaked through small inter-dimensional rips all the time.

Kind of ironic that I used to make a living frying the suckers in traps but had come to find them extremely useful.

Ah, there. One was lurking on an apartment building within sight, about a block away. Probably hiding under one of the many awnings. I reached out more firmly, this time with the intent to control. My senses automatically zeroed in on the active point of the creature's mind. I carefully penetrated into it, trying not to cringe outwardly. I'd done this many dozens of times, but it was still unpleasant.

Taking command of the minor demon, I sent it into flight toward the Fairmont. It was a risk in broad daylight. If someone spotted it, they'd call the local Demon Patrol, and that would definitely tip off Damien.

I steered the demon to the top of the hotel and directed it to make a lazy spiral, peering into each window as it passed. Using my necro vision, I watched through the creature's eyes.

The shades were drawn over many of the windows, and the top couple of floors yielded nothing useful.

About midway down, the creature passed a window just as a man appeared in it to yank a curtain across.

My breath stilled, and I pushed away from the side of the office building.

I knew that face. It was the dark-eyed guy in Damien's photos.

I used the minor demon to figure out what floor Damien's ex was on while I squeezed my eyes closed and tried to tame my spinning thoughts.

I sent out a fierce prayer that Damien was up there with my brother. Or, maybe he'd already handed Evan over to the mages and this was the victory celebration? No. Damien wouldn't still be hanging out here if he'd given up my brother. He'd be with his family, basking in the glow of their approval and making up for all those lost years as the outcast black sheep of the Stein family. It seemed that not even the prospect of reuniting with an old love would keep him from that. I didn't think so anyway. Though Damien's ex *was* pretty hot.

I had to try to talk Damien out of it. No one else was going to ensure Evan's safety. Zarella might, for a time, but I didn't want to rely on him. If Evan was up there, then I was extremely lucky to have found him, and I had to move now to try to convince Damien not to hand Evan over to the Steins. I had no idea what traps Damien might have waiting, or what he'd do to me, but I had to take the chance.

Turning to the reaper within me and the faint whisper of the *in-between*, I faded from the realm of the living. The glass doors of the Fairmont didn't exist in limbo land, so I walked right into the hotel lobby. Damien's ex was on the eighth floor. I passed the elevator and found the stairs. With hellhound-ghost Loki following me and the gray mist puffing up around my legs, I took the stairs two at a time.

On floor eight, I exited the stairwell and took a moment to orient myself.

Damn. The room doors were solid. You never knew what you'd get in the *in-between*. Sometimes doors carried over, and sometimes they didn't.

I navigated though the hallway until I was fairly sure I'd reached the right room. I couldn't be certain because I was estimating the location from an external view.

Now what? I could wait for housekeeping and then slip in when the door was open. But odds were Damien wasn't letting anyone in at all.

What were my options? I could pull the fire alarm, but Damien would just vanish with Evan. I needed the element of surprise, but not to the point that Damien would attack or disappear. I went to the door to the right of Damien's room and released my connection with the *in-between*. I planned to knock, flash back to limbo land when someone answered, go through the room and out the window, and hopefully find a ledge or something that would allow me to hop over to

Damien's window. Then I could sneak in, pop into the living realm, and . . . well, I wasn't sure exactly how I'd get Damien to listen to me, but something would come to me.

In the land of the living, I reflexively touched the pouch on my belt that held my chain whip. It was much heavier than my old weapon, but I found the weight reassuring. Plus, the metal made a faint rattle when I walked, which made me feel like a badass Old West cowboy with spurs ready for a shootout.

I took a deep breath and raised my hand to knock on the door. Just before my knuckles made contact, there was some noise on the other side, the handle unlatched with a click, and the door whooshed inward.

My heart jumped into my throat as I recognized Damien's ex. He was looking back over his shoulder and saying something, one hand on the door and the other holding the ice bucket.

I had a split second to react. I grabbed the end of my whip with one hand, lunged forward and caught the guy in a chokehold with the other arm, and kicked the door closed behind me with my heel. Loki whined in the hallway, put out that he'd been closed off.

Some part of my mind registered that the guy had no magical ability. The rest of my attention was on Damien.

He'd taken a step toward us, but then he stopped and stood calmly with his feet planted wide and his arms at his sides.

"Really, Ella?" Damien tsked softly. "He doesn't even have any magic. He's no threat to you."

My pulse raced and my breath came fast as a new surge of adrenaline coursed through me.

Even from several feet away, I could see the pinpoint lights in Damien's eyes, like two little star fields trapped there. The eyes of a mage.

I couldn't see Evan but guessed he was on the bed, which I assumed was to the left of where Damien stood. The TV on the wall to his right was playing on mute.

"Evan?" I called, edging to the right to try to see if he was on the bed. "Are you okay?"

No response.

"We need to talk, Damien," I said, returning my attention to my former partner. "In fact, I insist. You don't want me to hurt your friend, do you? I know you still care about him."

I flicked my wrist, sending earth, air, and fire magic into my chain whip. It made a satisfying metallic noise as it snaked up and around the man I held. In a blink, Damien's ex was bound from ankles to shoulders with his arms pinned to his sides. Still palming the whip's handle, I pulsed a little more fire into the metal, just enough to be uncomfortable. The guy winced and let out a cry through clenched teeth. Between the heat and the razor edges of the links, all it would take was one twitch from me to leave him with a hundred slices.

Damien didn't even glance at him. My heart plummeted.

Shit. This wasn't going at all the way I'd hoped.

I had a split-second warning when his face twitched. On reflex, I faded to the *in-between* just as a blob of white mage magic large enough to engulf me hurled through the air. Damien could do a dozen awful things with his newfound magic—paralyze my body, fry my brain, crush me into a tiny pinpoint of matter. I didn't know what he'd intended with the blast, and I didn't want to find out.

In limbo land, I sprang forward, getting a running start, and then popped back into the land of the living just in time to ram into Damien. The shock of the surprise worked. His magic faltered, and we went crashing to the floor. I flashed back into the *in-between*, slammed my forearms together to connect the pearlescent markings around them, and reached for the magic flowing through the nearest ley line.

Pulling the magic back with me into the living realm sent a lightning bolt of pain through my head and down my spine. But I held on, sending it out though my fingertips as I gripped Damien's neck.

In the weeks since he'd disappeared, I'd discovered more about the nature of the silver magic from the *in-between*, the power that did not belong in the living realm. It was a sort of death magic. It carved away at living souls.

I glanced off to the side. My brother was there on the bed, sitting up and watching us with a glassy expression.

"Evan, get up!" I screamed at him. "Get up and run!"

He just blinked vacantly. It was then that I noticed the medical supplies on the nightstand—syringes and small glass vials.

Fury shot through me, fueling my magic, as my gaze whipped back down to Damien.

"It's not what you think," he choked out, his nails scrabbling at my hands as he tried to pry my fingers from his neck. "I'm not drugging him. I'm helping him get clean."

"Why should I believe you?" I demanded.

I pulled more silver magic, and my head screamed.

"Because I have no reason to lie about that," he whispered harshly.

Probably true. Damien no longer cared whether I thought he was a good person.

I pulled more power. Dark blotches began to invade my vision.

"I'm leaving, and I'm taking my brother with me," I said, my voice little more than a growl through the pain.

Damien's eyes tightened with fear as the death magic continued to flow through him. For a moment I thought he might beg for mercy. Stupid me.

"No," he said. "You're not."

White light blinded me, and the force of mage magic punched me so hard I flew backward through the air.

I had just enough time for the fleeting anticipation of how badly it was going to hurt when my head slammed into the wall or the door. Still surrounded by sheer white, I crashed into a solid surface with such agonizing force, I figured it might kill me.

I wanted to call my brother's name, but I passed out instead.

Damien's blow didn't kill me, of course. I had the soul of the reaper Xaphan riding around with me, and it wouldn't let me die—not easily, anyway. But when I came to, I wished I were dead.

I had no idea how long I'd been lying there in a heap on the hotel room floor. There was insistent knocking at the door, but I couldn't do more than blink and groan. Then there was snuffling in my face, soft whines, and a wet tongue lapping at my ear.

"Hey, boy," I whispered to Loki. I had no idea how he'd managed to get inside the room, but at least he hadn't been hurt.

Tears sprang to my eyes when I tried to roll to my side. My brain felt like it needed to explode through my ears or it'd drive me mad with the pain and pressure. I stayed where I was for several seconds, the sensations in my body too excruciating to even force out a moan. The knocking at the door ceased, to my enormous relief.

I drew a slow breath and cracked my eyelids open. In my periphery, I spotted a smear of maroon. At first I thought it was the strange magic that I sometimes left in a trail, but the sticky sheen and metallic scent told me it was blood.

With deliberate, careful movements, I sat up and touched the side of my head where the pain seemed to radiate the worst. I immediately wished I hadn't. My hair was matted with blood, and there was a huge goose egg where my skull had hit. Using the wall for support, I rose to my feet and then stood there fighting back nausea brought on by the motion of standing.

I didn't have to look, I knew the room was empty. Damien, his ex, and my brother were gone. I'd used up my chance to save Evan, and my old partner had nearly killed me for my trouble. I'd probably never be able to find Damien on my own now.

As I shifted my gaze down to my hellhound-doodle, I caught sight of myself in the closet's mirror doors a couple of feet away.

"Oh, my god," I said to my reflection. "You look like you got stuffed down a kitchen sink drain with the food grinder turned on."

I had the beginnings of not one, but two black eyes, my lip was split and had bled all over the lower half of my face, and my hair was a matted disaster.

I looked down at my dog. "I don't suppose you saw which way Damien went?"

He cocked his head at me and then panted with his tongue out.

"Yeah, I didn't think so." I pushed away from the wall, testing my balance. "It's not your fault. He probably did that mage thing and just disappeared into thin air. Pretty damn inconvenient for us, huh?"

I stood there breathing slowly and testing each limb, trying to focus on the fact that if not for my reaper giving me the ability to withstand bad injuries and heal quickly from them, I probably *would* be dead. But it was challenging to summon up much gratitude when it felt like every bone in my body had been beaten until it cracked.

My spirits lifted a little when I spotted my chain whip on the floor. I wasn't surprised Damien had left it. He was confident he could beat me, and allowing me to keep my prized weapon was just another way of showing it. Moving like an arthritic octogenarian, I bent and picked up the handle, carefully looping the razor-edged chains so I could drop it into the pouch on my belt. I was so focused on the task that when my phone buzzed in my pocket I nearly pitched into the wall again. I pulled it out and answered.

"Hey, Deb," I said, trying my damnedest to make my voice sound normal. I even tried to force the scowl from my face and replace it with something more pleasant, but it hurt too much to shift my expression.

There was a gasp. "Ella, what happened?" Deb asked.

I cleared my throat. "Uh, nothing. Why?"

She snorted. "Because you sound like someone punched you in the throat. Also, I'm an empath, remember?"

"Oh yeah," I said tiredly.

"Are you okay?"

"Uhhh." I lifted a hand and shrugged one shoulder, as if she could see me. "Relative to what?"

"*Ella.*"

"I had a little run-in with Damien."

She gasped again. "Oh, no. Did he have Evan?"

"Yeah, but they got away while I was uncon—um, yeah, they escaped," I said, silently berating myself. I didn't want to upset Deb. She had more than enough on her mind already, and she didn't need to be worrying about me getting beat up and knocked out with mage magic.

"Where are you?"

"San Francisco."

She sighed. "I'm so sorry they got away, Ella."

I closed my eyes and ran my hand down my face, and instantly regretted touching the bruises.

"I'll keep after him," I said. "Is everything okay there?"

"Um, yeah, I'm fine. I was just trying to figure out where you were."

"Oh, shit, the coven meeting," I said. I nearly smacked my forehead but stopped myself just in time.

"Sorry. I know it seems trivial compared to everything else."

"Nah, I'll be home in ten minutes. Wait for me?"

"Of course," she said. She gave a little laugh. "I still can't wrap my mind around you jumping from place to place the way you do through the *in-between*. You could travel the world for free!"

"Ha, maybe someday," I said. "See you soon."

"Okay, see you soon."

We hung up, and I went to the bathroom and stripped off my rumpled, bloodied clothes. I didn't have time to wash them or buy new ones, but I could at least get the blood out of my hair and off my face, so I'd look slightly less like a horror movie victim when I arrived home. Deb wasn't squeamish, but nobody wanted to see their best friend covered in their own blood.

As hot water cascaded down my beat-up body, the emotions I'd been keeping in check flooded through me. Frustration and anger were enough to keep tears in check, but my gut wrenched every time I recalled my brother's vacant face.

When was the last time Evan laughed or did something he actually enjoyed? Certainly not while he'd been trapped in the vampire feeder den. Even before he'd disappeared, he was already in trouble. I still held onto hope that someday he'd have a real life, normal days where he woke up coherent and spent his time on something productive, something he was actually engaged and interested in. It was hard to imagine, though. He'd been used for so many years, and if Damien's family and the other powerful mages got their hands on Evan, they'd sacrifice him to close the interdimensional rips that had been unleashing chaos on our world for decades.

I squeezed my eyes closed, trying to block out the hurt. It compacted, sinking into my gut and hanging there like a lead baseball.

I turned off the shower, quickly dried off and mopped as much water out of my hair as I could, and then got dressed. I plugged the sink and turned on the water, twisting my damp hair up into a bun while I waited for the basin to fill.

There was only one option left: beg Phillip Zarella to help me find Evan. I'd hoped it wouldn't come to that. I didn't want the madman's help, and definitely didn't want to contemplate what he'd want in return, but Zarella and his connections were my only chance. A shiver crept over my scalp and down my neck as I contemplated using an army of zombies, demons, and who knew what else to save my brother.

The sink nearly full, I shut off the flow of water. Tuning into the faint, ever-present tug of the *in-between*, I faded into the land of gray and mist. Loki followed, and I used the water to take us to the dish of water my neighbor left out next to the dish of food for stray cats on her porch.

I went to my own door and stood there for a moment as tiny dots of white fell from the sky, a barely-there dusting of snow. The lights were on inside, and I knew Deb was waiting for me, but suddenly I felt so heavy I wasn't sure if I'd be able to force my legs to carry me forward.

Loki nudged my hand, as if knowing I needed a little encouragement.

I forced my feet to move. "Glad to be home, boy?"

The hellhound-doodle gave a little yip.

"Yeah, me too," I whispered.

Deb opened the door before I could reach for the knob.

She let out a little shriek. "Ella! Your aura looks like hell, and your face—oh my god, your poor face." She started to reach up to touch my temple but then pulled her hand back.

"I know, I know," I said. My insides warmed at her concern, even though I didn't want her to get upset. "I'll be fine."

I closed the door behind me. When I turned around, she was standing with her hands on her hips and an accusing look pinching her face.

"You used death magic," she said. "A lot of it."

"I had to. And for a second, I actually had the upper hand against Damien. Or maybe I just thought I did. I don't even know at this point." I smoothed my hands over my head, pushing back stray tendrils of hair and trying to recall that moment when I was sure I'd seen fear in his eyes as death magic streamed into him, attacking his soul. Or had I just wanted to see vulnerability so badly I'd misinterpreted it?

"How bad?" Deb demanded.

"My head is pounding, but I'm okay," I said. "I can wait until after the meeting to get healed."

She peered at me for a moment. "The minute we're done, you go straight to Gina," she said, relenting.

"Yes, ma'am."

"How did he look? Evan?" She'd gone to get her purse from the table next to the sofa but stilled, watching me as she waited for my response.

I sighed. "Not great, but not terrible, I guess. Damien claimed he was getting Evan clean. There were syringes and stuff next to the bed."

Deb turned to me, her face softening into a mix of sadness and concern. I had to look away as a lump rose in my throat.

"You're going to get him back," she said firmly. "I'm sure of it."

I pulled my lips in and bit down, unable to respond.

"You sure you're okay to go?" she asked.

I cleared my throat and nodded. "Yeah, let's get on with it."

I'd almost said *let's get it over with*, but I caught myself just in time. Deb was still under the influence of Lynnette's charisma and promises of financial security, and even though I didn't trust the coven leader with a bucket of dead rats, let alone my best friend's future, criticizing Lynnette in the past had only driven a wedge between me and Deb.

Deb and I went out to my old pickup, and I got behind the wheel. I waited until she had her safety belt on, the lap part tucked under her growing belly, before pulling away from the curb.

"Guess what?" Deb asked, her voice an odd mix of subtle emotions I couldn't quite read.

"What?"

"The divorce will be final by the end of next week, unless Keith decides to put up a fuss about something."

"Hallelujah!" I crowed and then quickly glanced at her. "I mean, that's good, right?"

She nodded and blew out a long breath. "Yeah, it's time. I'm ready."

"What's going to happen after the baby comes?" I asked. "Is Keith going to try to be involved?"

"Our agreement says I'll have full custody," she said. "It helped a lot that he's currently jobless and his employment record is pretty crappy."

"That's such a relief," I said, truly glad that she would have full legal control.

"If he wants to be part of his child's life, he's going to have to make an effort," Deb said, turning solemn. "And we both know what he's like when it comes to committing to something."

I couldn't quite tell whether she was hoping her soon-to-be-ex would or wouldn't make an attempt to be a father to the baby.

"Well, one thing's for sure," I said, steering onto the street that would take us away from the heart of downtown and up to Lynnette's neighborhood. "You're going to be an amazing mom. The best."

Deb reached over and patted my arm. "And you're going to be an awesome auntie. And godmother."

My eyes widened, and I flicked a look at her before returning my attention to the road. "What?"

She gave a shrug and a little smile. "Who else would I pick? You're my family. You always have been."

"Aw, Deb, you're going to make me cry," I said, for once sincere about my emotions. I blinked back tears for, what, the third time that day?

Then it occurred to me that Deb could have chosen Lynnette as the baby's godmother. In covens it was common practice to do such a thing. That sobered me up.

We talked about the baby, and Deb chattered happily all the way to Lynnette's. But my mind was already jumping ahead to the coven meeting, trying to guess the possible manipulations the coven leader would have in store for us this week.

Lynnette leblanc lived in a large house built primarily in the Victorian style with a few modern touches. By my standards, it was a mansion, especially considering she lived there alone. I couldn't help questioning whether she could still afford the mortgage, considering the recent hit to her income. She'd pissed off a dragon oracle that lived in a different dimension by trying to steal some of the dragon's magic. As penance, she'd lost her talent of exorcism, a service that had been in high demand and for which she'd charged large sums.

In fact, her exorcist services had been so unique it had been the foundation of the coven when the group first formed. She'd commanded extravagant fees that had allowed her to fund the start of the coven.

As I parked the truck along the curb in front of the hedge that marked the line between Lynnette's yard and her neighbors, I wondered if any of the other witches in the coven had considered how truly negatively Lynnette's recent actions had affected the group. Before I was coerced into joining, the coven had actually been complete in its membership. But Lynnette's dabblings with rip magic had indirectly led to the death of Amanda, one of the original members. I'd filled the opening. Since then, Lynnette had created more trouble, but she was cunning in how she dealt with the other women, and they never seemed to hold her accountable for her transgressions. Her charisma and ability to seek out and exploit the thing each witch most wanted in life helped fuel the intense loyalty that already existed in the coven.

This was one of the reasons part of me hoped things would eventually work out between Deb and Detective Lagatuda. It wasn't that I wanted my best friend to rush into another serious relationship, but Deb's deep longing for family—even an improvised one—had drawn her to the coven and held her there. If she had an actual family, maybe she wouldn't be so emotionally reliant on the coven. That was my hope, anyway.

And that was where Lynnette had the upper hand with Deb. I could provide her with friendship and support, but I was only one person. Lynnette offered a tightknit group of women, twelve ready-made sisters who vowed lifelong loyalty to each other.

The others were arriving, too, and a handful of us trooped up the front walk to Lynnette's door. She opened it and invited us in with a smile. Dressed in her usual black clothes, calf-high Doc Martens, and with heavy eyeliner and her midnight hair twisted into an intricate braid that fell halfway down her back, she was the very picture of goth chic.

Her demeanor cooled slightly when her eyes fell on me. "Hi, Ella," she said.

I gave her a nod but didn't try to fake pleasantries. She'd come to my aid more than once recently, and she professed to want to help me, but Lynnette never seemed to do anything unless there was something in it for her.

Since I was more powerful than she was—at least in straight-up magical ability, if not yet in skill—our dynamic had become even more antagonistic. But very little of it was out in the open. It simmered beneath the surface of her serene, maroon-lipsticked smile, and she was way too shrewd to show her true animosity in front of the other women.

Jennifer, a very rare vampire-witch, came forward and grasped one of Deb's hands, towing her toward the overstuffed crimson velvet chair that was considered the prime seat in Lynnette's living room.

"What's up, mama-to-be?" Jen asked. "How're you feeling?"

The other women milled around Deb as she sat down and updated them on the last doctor visit, which had been a couple of days prior, and I had to admit their interest and concern were very sweet. Aside from being too susceptible to their leader's manipulations, I had no real objections to any of the women aside from Lynnette. They all seemed like decent people.

"The divorce will be final soon, too," Deb said.

Lynnette stepped into the group, and the others automatically moved to make space for her.

"We'll have to celebrate," she said, beaming at Deb. "This is a big year for you."

Deb pressed her lips together and then smiled. "Sure is. Lots of changes."

"We're here for you, no matter what," the coven leader said with a little tilt of her head and a pat on Deb's shoulder.

Deb nodded. "You know I appreciate all of you. This coven means the world to me."

Lynnette shot me a saccharine smile through the crowd. I ground my teeth as anger spiked like thorns inside me, and my entire head seemed to heat up. I knew my reaction was overblown, but I was spent—magically and emotionally— from the confrontation with Damien and being so close to Evan only to have him slip away again.

And then I saw red. Literally, the world became awash in blood. I inhaled sharply, but no one noticed as their attention was still on Deb.

Oh, *shit*.

I pressed my fingertips to my temples and squeezed my eyes closed. Was this it? Had I pushed my magic too far? Was I going to keel over onto Lynnette's luxurious rug, dead of an aneurism?

I braced for agony, ready to call out for help. But the pain didn't come. Slowly, I opened my eyes and peered around.

The world was still red, but I wasn't dead. In fact, I felt pretty damn good. Except for the odd throbbing in my hands.

I looked down and found my fingers and palms bathed in concentrated clouds of the maroon magic. Tiny sparks lit in it, sending soft shivers along my skin. I turned my hands over, staring at the way it moved with my motion, like fat, pulsating mittens of magic.

"Ella, what the crap is *that*?" Jen's alarmed voice drew my eyes up.

All the women were staring at me. I was suddenly acutely aware of their hearts, and their individual pulses seemed to form a little cacophony of faint drumbeats.

"What?" Deb rose from the chair in alarm. "What is it?"

Jen's brows lifted. "You can't see it, can you?" she asked Deb.

My best friend shook her head.

"Can any of you see it?" Jen looked around at the women. She returned her gaze to me. "It's that blood-red magic."

Her eyes were gleaming in a way that made me a little uncomfortable. Her upper lip twitched, her teeth baring for a moment. Jen was a docile vamp, a victim of the VAMP2 virus, but with a special implant that was required by law. The tiny device calmed her natural bloodlust and allowed her to walk in sunlight unharmed. But something about the maroon-toned magic pulsing around my hands seemed to be affecting her, and I didn't like it.

On instinct, I sent my focus downward into the ground and pulled earth magic. Green strands of power snaked up and around me. I directed the magic down my arms to my hands, and it snuffed out the blood-red magic.

Jen blinked several times and sucked in a sharp breath through her nose. No one else seemed to notice her brief but strange little episode.

Lynnette folded her arms and thrust out one hip. "Everything okay over there?" she asked, clearly irritated that she'd lost control of the group's attention.

I gave her a serene smile. "Just peachy." I raised a palm in a carry-on gesture, which only seemed to agitate her more.

Everyone shifted around finding places to sit, and Lynnette started talking. My mind was still on the maroon magic. I slid a glance at Jen, thinking about her reaction. I'd seen the magic before. I sometimes left trails of it, and Rogan had as well. I'd thought it an odd sort of footprints-in-the-sand phenomenon of reapers who walked among the living, not as a magic that could be wielded. But as it had pulsed around my hands and sent tiny sparks lighting and dying, I knew it wasn't just a passive artifact. And I was suddenly just as sure that it had something to do with blood.

I suddenly itched for privacy so I could try to summon it again. There was something darkly alluring about the feel of the crimson magic. Warm and vital, yet dangerous.

Feeling eyes on me, I looked up to meet Lynnette's gaze. Curiosity flickered in her dark eyes, and I knew she was thinking about the blood-red magic, too, even though she hadn't been able to see it.

Wait. That was wrong. She *had* seen it. Lynnette, like me and Jen, was death-touched. I didn't know the story of how it happened to Lynnette, but her former power of exorcism was proof of it. I would bet my entire payout from the construction site job that she'd seen it but had just kept quiet. As a power-hungry collector of magics, she was probably as eager to see it again as I was. But she'd want to figure out a way to take some of it and keep it for herself. I didn't understand the methods she used to sample and store magic that wasn't hers, but I knew she did it.

I narrowed my eyes as her glance slid away from me and skipped across the rest of the women. Perhaps I could find a way to use Lynnette's desire to my advantage.

". . . and I've saved the best and most important announcement for last," she was saying. She paused dramatically. "We've been granted our coven charter. Our membership is sealed and we're official!"

Gasps, squeals, and excited chatter filled the room. I swallowed sourly. I'd planned to find a way to get out of the coven before the charter went through, but leaving a coven wasn't a simple thing to do. I hadn't figured out how to break my ties, let alone persuade Deb to leave with me, and now I was truly stuck.

Deb leaned over, throwing one arm around my shoulders. She was smiling with tears in her eyes. Her joy faltered a little when she caught sight of my face. I forced a weak grin.

Maybe it was better that I hadn't found a way out. It would have devastated her if I'd quit the coven. I stood and hugged the other women, trying to focus on the fact that I genuinely liked them rather than the feeling of being shackled to Lynnette.

"Okay, we'll have a little ceremony and celebration at the end, but for now let's wrap up our business," Lynnette called over the din. She started going through the coven financials.

When she paused, obviously ready to move on to a different topic, I straightened.

"Hey, what happened to that mysterious investor you talked about?" I asked. "You haven't mentioned it lately. We should get the money now that the charter is sealed, right?"

Over a month ago, I'd forced her to confess to the coven that her actions—tearing small rips in order to harvest the neon blue magic around them—had ended up getting Amanda killed. But Lynnette had managed to one-up me by immediately announcing that an anonymous investor had contacted her, offering to sponsor the coven with a wad of money. The only catch was that the person insisted the current membership be kept as it was, which meant that if

I'd left I'd have screwed the group out of cash. Most covens ended up financially failing in their first couple of years. If that happened, they lost their charter. She'd basically trapped me in the coven and distracted the women from the confession of her transgression in one fell swoop.

Lynnette's face twitched. "I expect the first payment within the week," she said evenly.

I gave a little shake of my head and held back a scoff. "So, you've been in contact with the investor?"

She gave me a serene smile. "Of course."

"But you still don't know who it is." It was more a statement than a question, and my tone conveyed my doubt.

A couple of the women looked back and forth between me and Lynnette. The mood had shifted, becoming slightly less jubilant.

The coven leader spread her hands. "The person insisted on anonymity."

"So how are you contacting him or her?" I asked.

"Through an attorney."

"Ah. Okay. Well, it will certainly be exciting when we get that payment."

I didn't believe her, and she knew it. If there was really an anonymous angel donor, I'd eat a bowl of Loki's dog food.

When we took a break, I stood and moved a little away from the group. As much as I wanted to prove Lynnette wrong, I had bigger concerns. I pulled out my phone and sent a message to the email address Phillip Zarella had given me to use when I needed to contact him.

Damien may have already handed Evan over to the Steins. We need to move while they can still be stopped.

I was asking for Zarella's help but didn't want to say it outright. Besides, Zarella and his cronies had their own reasons for wanting to keep my brother free. Evan was the key to closing the rips—all of them—permanently. Jacob Gregori, the Steins, and the Order of Mages were all in agreement that this was so. My parents had thought Evan himself might grow up to seal the rips, but that wasn't how it worked, apparently. Evan wouldn't wield the magic. He would channel the magic of the mages, and in the process, he'd die.

The only problem was, doing it would mean my brother sacrificing his life. Zarella and other like-minded people didn't want the rips closed. They thrived on chaos and darkness, and they believed that demons, the new vampire and zombie viruses, and the various magics the rips had unleashed all had a rightful place in our world. I didn't agree, but because I didn't want my brother to die, Zarella and I were uneasy allies in trying to keep Evan from falling into the hands of either Jacob Gregori or the mages.

I didn't admit that I'd found Damien but spooked him into relocating again. I suspected Zarella already knew. He had eyes everywhere—literally, as he used demons, zombies, and who-knew-what-else as his personal spies even while he was confined to the Gregori Industries campus, hiding out from the authorities and the rest of the world. Zarella had tried to bully me, and since I'd screwed things up, I half expected him to take more severe measures. Maybe even try to have me killed. But Zarella was probably my last hope for saving Evan, so I'd have to convince the madman that we were still on the same side. I needed leverage.

Someone touched the back of my arm, and I tensed, thinking it was Lynnette. But when I turned, I found Deb peering up at me, her forehead lined with concern.

"Everything okay?" she asked. "I know Evan is on your mind, and you have every right to be preoccupied by what's going on, but is there something else?"

Crap. She'd definitely picked up on my disapproval of Lynnette. I probably should have kept my mouth shut, but I was too fatigued to muster up much self-control. I tried to let the tension ease out of my shoulders.

"Just a lot to juggle," I said. I gave her a crooked smile. "You know better than anyone else how that goes."

"I know you're worried about what Damien is going to do," she said. "But I don't think he's completely gone. I think there's still a good person in there, and he'll come to his senses about Evan."

My smile turned sad. I appreciated her sense of optimism, but I couldn't imagine she was right.

"We can hope," I said.

Lynnette and a couple of the other women emerged from the kitchen carrying trays of tiny desserts, champagne flutes, and two bottles of expensive bubbly. I fought the urge to roll my eyes. How much had all of that cost? It had most certainly come out of the coven's collective income.

She filled the glasses, which got passed around. Deb didn't take one, foregoing alcohol during her pregnancy, though she loved champagne.

"Before we toast, I just want to mention one more thing," Lynnette said. "Now that we're chartered, we need to officially fill the roles of Keeper of Records, Keeper of Means, and Keeper of Ritual. Before you leave tonight, we'll take nominations."

My brows lifted. I was surprised she was pushing us to do nominations so soon. Lynnette, as coven leader, was automatically granted the leading role of Moon Priestess. Keeper of Means was basically a treasurer, and Keeper of Records was a secretarial position.

I leaned over to whisper to Deb. "Nominate me for Keeper of Means."

If I were elected, I would have full access to every bit of coven financial information. I could look for misconduct or, as I suspected with the supposed angel donor, outright lies in the financial records.

She gave me a surprised look, but then her expression turned pleased. "Of course I will. If you'll nominate me for Keeper of Ritual?"

It was my turn to be surprised. Keeper of Ritual was like the vice president of the coven, second in power to the Moon Priestess and authorized to take over her duties if she were absent or incapacitated. It was a little out of character for Deb to want such a position of authority, but I kind of liked that she had such an ambition.

"Absolutely," I said. "I might even vote for you."

"Gee, thanks." She gave me a wry look.

Holding our champagne, we gathered into a circle in the middle of the living room. Lynnette said a few words and then ended with a prayer to the elements for good fortune to shine upon the coven. It was shorter and less dramatic than usual, only adding to my feeling that she was trying to hurry things along.

"Okay, now grab some desserts and let's begin the nominations," she directed. "Anyone want to nominate a sister for Keeper of Ritual?"

My hand shot up. "I nominate Deb."

There were several murmurs of approval, and someone seconded.

Someone else nominated Marta, whose dyed-black hair and kohl eyeliner were an obvious imitation of Lynnette's goth chic look. I'd never had much to say to Marta, and vice-versa.

"Any more?" Lynnette asked, looking around the room. "Okay, what about nominations for Keeper of Means?"

"I nominate Ella," Deb called out.

Jen nominated Elena.

A few of the women looked surprised, but no one appeared disapproving, and a couple of people seconded. Someone nominated a petite blond named Becky, and I winced. If I remembered correctly, she had an accounting background.

Jen was the sole nomination for Keeper of Records.

"Wait, I need to change," Elena piped up. Marta, who was sitting next to Elena, had been whispering urgently in her ear. "Remove my nom for Keeper of Means."

Jen shot her a confused look.

"With that, we'll close nominations," Lynnette said, totally ignoring the subtext that seemed to be swirling between Marta, Elena, and Jen. "Next meeting, we'll vote."

My brows lifted again. It all seemed so abrupt. But as Lynnette ended the meeting, I didn't have time to ponder her motives any further. My phone was buzzing every couple of seconds, alerting me to an incoming message. As the group began to break up for the night, I peeked at the phone's screen. There was an email from Zarella.

The email contained two words—let's talk—followed by a phone number and the code name Alois. It was the number for another one of Zarella's many burner phones.

As I looked down at the screen, something dripped onto it.

"Shit," I mumbled when I realized it was a drop of blood.

I dug in my jacket pocket for a tissue. I'd taken to carrying around at least a couple of them because my nose was a faucet leaking crimson these days. Trying to angle myself away from Deb, I swiped blood off the phone and then pinched my nose with the tissue.

"Ella," said a stern voice at my shoulder. "You need to call Gina. *Now*."

Deb was there, standing with her hands planted on her hips. I knew she was trying to look authoritative, but she was mostly just adorable, with her pregnant tummy, rosy cheeks, and waves of strawberry blond hair loose around her shoulders. Her face was pinched and worried, though, and I knew she was right. I was playing a dangerous game, pushing the magic as hard as I had against Damien. And it wouldn't be the last time I forced it past healthy limits.

I nodded. "I'll call her right now and see if she can do a walk-in."

Deb's expression eased a little bit.

I dialed the magical healer. I knew it was Gina's off hours, but she was aware of my situation and often agreed to see me at odd times. Her services weren't cheap, but they were just about the only thing keeping my brain from dissolving to mush under the influence of the *in-between's* silver magic.

"I'm actually downtown setting up my new clinic space," she said. "Come here, and I'll do a session."

She gave me the address, and we hung up.

Deb was still hovering.

"She's going to see me now," I said. "She's downtown, so I'll drop you at home and then go."

My best friend's face relaxed, and she let her arms fall to her sides. "That's great. Please tell her thank you for doing it on such short notice."

In the past, Deb had forced me to go to healing sessions when I'd tried to brush off her concerns. But I no longer resisted. I would have contacted Gina even without Deb's prompting, because I knew a battle loomed ahead and I was going to need every shred of strength I could muster up.

I glanced at Zarella's message again. I'd try calling him from the truck once Deb was safe at home and I had some privacy.

Deb was subdued on the way home, her eyelids already drooping. She was getting tired earlier and earlier as her pregnancy progressed, and we were coming up on her bedtime. In front of the fourplex that housed our apartment, I waited for her to go in and shut the door before driving away. A block from home, I pulled over and tapped the number Zarella had given me.

My breath stilled as I listened to it ring. After about a dozen rings, I gave up and headed downtown. I couldn't keep Gina waiting.

Her new clinic space turned out to be in the same historic building that housed the bar I used to frequent when I was still on Demon Patrol. It was one of the favorite watering holes of all divisions of Supernatural Crimes. The first floor was a restaurant and the bar, the next two floors up were businesses, and then the rest of the upper floors were apartments. I'd tried to get one of them years ago, but they were the only apartments located in the middle of downtown, so someone practically had to die before they became available.

I passed the bar, went into the middle entrance of the building, and then took the stairs up to the second floor. The businesses were all closed, and the hallways were dark. At

Gina's suite, I rapped on the door. She answered, and I caught sight of boxes scattered around behind her.

A solidly-built woman a couple of inches shorter than me, Gina was both a conventional nurse and a magical healer.

She looked at the air around me, the way Deb sometimes did, checking out my aura.

"You've recently exerted yourself rather severely," she said, assessing rather than accusing.

"Guilty." I crooked a smile at her. There was no reason to try to deceive her about it. I looked around the space as she let me in. "Am I single-handedly funding this move, or what?"

She gave a little laugh, reaching back to sweep her thick, coarse hair up into a bun.

"Not quite," she said. "But my practice has been expanding, and I've outgrown the home-based setup."

I followed her into a smaller room, and she gestured at what was clearly intended to be a treatment area. In the center of the space there was a massage table I knew well.

I lay down face-up, and Gina dimmed the lights part way and went to work. Feather-light touches of magic brushed me from head to toe as she assessed the areas and extent of the damage. My eyelids drifted shut under the soothing sensation.

After about five minutes, her magic receded.

"Did Deb do some work on you already?" she asked.

I opened my eyes. "No, I won't let her do it anymore. I want her to conserve her energy for the rest of the pregnancy."

Gina was peering at me with a curious expression. "I could tell that you'd dangerously overextended yourself, but the damage is only about half what I would have expected."

I gave her a wry look. "Does that mean I get a discount?"

She didn't laugh. Instead, she tilted her head. "Something is different."

A little zing of apprehension spiraled up my spine. "Different bad, or different good?"

"If the damage is less than it should be, it's a good thing," she said, but she didn't sound all that convinced. "Can you think of anything that's changed since I saw you last?"

The feel of the crimson magic pulsing against my palms, as if I held a live beating heart in each one, flooded back to me.

"Do you know anything about magic the color of blood?" I asked. "I know it's associated with death or being death-touched, but I don't know what it is or how to use it."

Her eyes tensed, becoming uneasy. "Sounds like maybe a lesser-known Old World magics. What's your experience with it?"

"It's just sort of appeared a few times," I said. "Most recently and most strongly earlier tonight."

She frowned. "It doesn't make sense that death-associated magic would have any restorative or protective effect. It must have been something else."

I closed my eyes again as she started the healing part of the session. She was extremely skilled at her trade, but I disagreed with her assessment. Several months back, I'd been dead for nearly twenty minutes. Ever since, I'd been walking around with a reaper clinging to my soul. I could pull magic from a place where the living weren't allowed. I had the talent of necromancy. There was a good chance I was the only person in the world with that exact configuration of oddities. If there was anyone who might be helped by blood-colored death magic, I was probably a good candidate.

It wasn't that I didn't believe the crimson magic was dangerous—hell, all magics could be dangerous, depending on how they were used—but I'd felt a delicious sort of . . . *affinity* for it when it had been wrapped around my hands. Even more than before, I wanted to explore it. Test it. Feel it more strongly.

Normally, I dozed while Gina did her work. But this time I was buzzing on the memory of the blood-red magic and the prospect of it having some sort of protective effect.

Gina finished the session, and I tried not to wince as I paid her. Since getting fired from Demon Patrol, I no longer had medical coverage and the full fees for healing came out of my pocket.

"You should sit here for a few minutes and let it settle," she said.

"Nah, I'm good," I said, hopping off the table. "Besides, it's late, and I don't want to keep you."

"Are you sure? There's still a lot of swirling energy."

I waved her off with a smile. "Thanks so much for seeing me this late."

I didn't exactly feel fantastic as dizziness tried to pull me off balance. But my head was no longer pounding, and I was antsy to try to reach Zarella again.

I touched the table with my fingertips, just to make sure I was steady. Gina saw it.

"Ella, I really think you should take just a minute."

"I'll be fine," I called over my shoulder as I exited her clinic.

I had to keep a firm hold on the handrail as I navigated down the few flights of stairs to the ground floor. Once outside, I took a deep breath of winter air, hoping it would ground me and wash away the churning sensation in my head. It didn't help much. The door to the bar opened as a couple of people exited, letting out the sounds of chatter and laughter and the aromas of pub food and beer.

I dug out my phone and forced my feet forward. Apparently, that was too much for my body to coordinate, because I misjudged the curb. Stumbling off the edge, I tried to catch myself before I went down, but I'd stepped onto a patch of ice in the gutter, which only made things worse. My phone flew from my hand as my arms wind-milled.

I had enough time to think about how bad it would be to slam my head against the pavement before my feet flew out from under me.

Wincing, I tensed against the coming impact. But instead of ice and asphalt, I slammed into a solid body. Strong arms wrapped across my back and around my waist.

"Caught ya," said a deep voice.

I looked up into the amused face of Caleb Montgomery, the handsome, rusty-haired Supernatural Special Forces guy with sparkling green eyes who'd invited me out when we were finishing up at the construction site job.

There was a little smattering of applause from a few passersby, and I realized that Caleb held me in a dip, as if we'd just finished a dance number and this was our final pose. He carefully levered me upright, planting his foot against mine so I wouldn't slide, and then kept a hold of my arms.

"I didn't see you inside," he said, and it took me a moment to realize he meant the bar.

I shook my head. "I wasn't in there. I came from upstairs."

His brows rose.

"Not an apartment," I said. "The healer I use has a clinic up there."

"Ah." He seemed glad about that clarification.

"Thanks for that," I said as he released my arms.

I twisted around, looking for my fallen phone. Bad idea. My head swam, and I nearly lost my balance again. Caleb grasped my elbow.

"Maybe you need a refund from that healer," he said, his tone joking but his eyes intent. "Seems like you're not quite right yet."

I blew out a breath and ran one hand down my face. "She's really good. It's not her fault. She told me I shouldn't rush off yet," I said. I wasn't sure why I was telling him those details. "Ugh, I don't know where my phone went."

His hand moved to the small of my back, and he guided me forward a few feet toward a big, vintage H3 Hummer parked at the curb. He took my wrist and planted my hand on the passenger door handle, wrapping his fingers around mine to make sure my grip was secured. His warm touch sent a pleasant little zing through me.

"You hang on, and I'll find your phone," he said. "Any idea where it might have gone?"

I pointed down the sidewalk with my free hand. "Down there somewhere, I think?"

He turned on the flashlight function on his own phone and began sweeping the little beam of light back and forth, searching. Then he dropped to one knee to peer under a parked compact car. He reached under it and then stood, raising his hand triumphantly.

He wiped it off across the front of his jacket and then handed it to me.

"Oh, thank you," I said with a sigh of relief, suddenly realizing that if I lost the phone I would have also lost the temporary number where I could reach Zarella.

"Why don't you sit down a sec?" he suggested, gesturing at the car I was clinging to.

I blinked at the Hummer. "Is this yours?"

"Yeah, my baby. I restored it myself." He patted the hood and then gently moved me aside so he could open the passenger door. "Here, get in."

I didn't have the strength to resist. And I was a little bit afraid I might drive off the road if I tried to get in my truck just yet.

I leaned back in the seat while Caleb went around to the driver's side, got in, and started the engine.

"Was it the job that drained you?" he asked. It took me a second to clue in to the fact he was asking about the construction site. In some ways that job seemed like ages ago.

I shook my head. "That wasn't much of a strain," I said.

"What happened?" he asked. He was leaning forward with his arms draped over the steering wheel, his head turned toward me and his eyes intent with genuine interest.

I sighed heavily. "It's a long story."

"I'm a pretty good listener."

I gave a short little laugh, a polite sound. Part of me wanted to unload everything—tell someone about Damien, Evan, San Francisco, all of it. But there were some things I couldn't talk about. Like the part about becoming buddies with the most notorious madman since the Nazis.

"C'mon," he said, gently insisting. "You've obviously got a lot on your mind. Does it have anything to do with the disappearance of your old partner?"

I wasn't sure how he'd heard about Damien, but I wasn't completely surprised. Caleb was fairly new to Boise, but he and many others probably knew that Damien and I had gone into business together after I was fired from Demon Patrol and he left voluntarily. And I couldn't exactly hide the fact that on the last several jobs awarded to our company, Perfect Circle Supernatural Services, I'd been the only one to show up for the work.

"In a way, yes," I admitted reluctantly.

"What happened there?" he asked. "Or is that prying too much?"

I turned to look at him. "I'm not trying to be cryptic, but you probably wouldn't even believe me if I told you."

He crooked a smile at me. "Maybe. How are you feeling now?"

"A little better," I said. "Thanks again for keeping me from cracking my skull open on the curb. And digging my phone out of the muck."

"No problem, Ella."

I liked the way my name sounded in his resonant voice. I liked that he seemed so *normal*. And kind. And really fricking hot, if I let myself focus on that.

"We should get together sometime," I blurted. I snapped my lips closed. Where the hell had that come from? The last thing I needed was to start dating. And I wasn't ready, anyway. At least, I hadn't thought so.

"I'd love that," he said sincerely. "This weekend?"

I couldn't back out now. I'd suggested it, after all. But I found I didn't want to back out. I needed something good to look forward to. Something normal. Something with sparkling green eyes and a ridiculously cute dimple.

"Sure, if I'm in town." And not dead from mage magic.

I gave him my number, and then there was a pause. I wasn't sure what else to say and didn't want it to become awkward, so I started to reach for the door handle.

He leaned in and touched my cheek with the tips of his fingers, and his lips brushed mine. It was a quick, soft kiss, with no demand or force, but somehow still electric. Warmth flooded through me, and I resisted the sudden urge to lean in for more. There was no need to rush. There was enough heat in his kiss to clearly convey the promise of more intensity. I savored the prospect of it, to my own surprise.

He pulled back a little, his eyes only inches from mine. "Just trying to distract you from your brooding thoughts."

I let out a little laugh. "It worked."

He got out of the car and came around to my side, clearly intending to walk me to my truck, which was just around the corner. He didn't try to hold my hand or anything, and I was fine with that.

Still buzzing on the feel of Caleb's lips, for a minute or two after I started my truck I nearly forgot about Zarella. At a stop light, I called the number he'd given me. It rang twice, and then there was a faint click.

"Hello, Ella," said the madman.

"Alois," I replied. He'd warned me to not ever use his real name in our conversations or correspondence.

Zarella tsked. "You shouldn't have gone to San Francisco, Ella."

I smothered a sigh at the back of my throat. "You heard about that, huh?"

"We had eyes on the boy," he said. "We were only waiting to find out when and where the mages plan to make their move. We had things under control."

I started to feel suitably repentant about rushing off so haphazardly. But then something suddenly occurred to me.

"Then why didn't you stop me? You could have, if you'd wanted to. You've got necromancers at your disposal. Probably some really powerful friends, too. Right?"

I couldn't quite put my finger on it, but something was pinging in my gut. Why *hadn't* Zarella stopped me from confronting Damien?

"You assume that would have been an easy thing to do," he said. "But you do not give yourself sufficient credit. I have powerful friends, yes, but no one with the ability to chase you between the realm of the living and the land where souls await the reaper's blade."

What he said might have been true, but I didn't completely buy the flattery.

"So now what?" I pressed. "Where did Damien fly off to? How are we going to keep him from giving Evan to his parents?"

He made a sad little humming sound. "I wish I could trust you with that information, but you've shown yourself to be too impulsive."

My chest clenched. "No, you *have* to tell me. He's my brother."

"We have a plan in place. All we need is the time and location of the planned sacrifice. If we need your assistance, we'll be in touch," Zarella said. "Until then, you shouldn't interfere, Ella."

"You'll be in touch?" I repeated incredulously. My breath was coming faster as my pulse sped in anger. "That's not how this works. You don't get to decide you'll *be in touch*."

On some level I realized what I was saying was absurd, that Zarella really did have all the power in this situation, but panic was gripping my heart with ice-cold fingers. I knew the madman could do whatever he wanted to, and there was hardly a damn thing I could do to stop him.

"Get a hold of yourself," he snapped. "And remember who you're talking to. You've failed over and over again on your own, remember? You need me, if you want any chance at saving your brother. I'll say it again, but only once more. Do. Not. Interfere. Goodbye, Ella."

Angry heat flooded up the back of my neck. "How dare you try to cut me out of this," I hissed into the phone. I knew he'd already disconnected, but I couldn't seem to stop myself from yelling. "I won't let you do it. He's not yours. Damn you, Zarella, don't hurt him!"

I slammed on the brakes and pulled over and then jammed the phone into the passenger seat before I tried to throw it through the windshield. I gripped the steering wheel, squeezing until my arms shook.

I wanted to kill Zarella. If he'd been there at that moment, I'd have tried to strangle him with my bare hands. His words hammered through my mind. There was truth to what he'd said, which only fueled my outrage.

My head began to throb, and my vision swam. I tried to calm myself, but my breath only became more ragged. Something wetted my upper lip, and I tasted blood. Maybe this would be the aneurism that ended me for good. The reaper helped me heal quickly from bodily injury and even protected me from dying under certain kinds of attack, but if blood vessels in my brain burst, I'd no longer be there, even if the reaper kept my body alive. I'd be a shell carrying the soul of Xaphan the reaper. Maybe they'd name a new kind of zombie after me.

All of those thoughts floated on the current of my anger, and when the hottest flash of it began to recede, I finally lifted my head and peeled my eyelids open.

The throbbing in my temples had calmed. My nose was no longer dripping blood. But my hands were bathed in sparking crimson.

I blinked down at them. Carefully, as though trying to avoid spooking a tiny bird, I lifted my arms until my palms were level with my eyes. The blood-red magic soothed me, somehow, surrounding me in warm velvet. Reaching out with my mind, as I did when I took control of demons using necromancy, I probed the pulsating magic. It responded by flowing over my arms, and up my chest. I inhaled sharply as it continued up my neck. It dulled, and afraid it would disappear, I forced myself to stay calm.

Like a living thing, the magic crept up my neck and over my head. Again, I had to tamp down my panic as it covered my eyes and flowed into my nose. I could still breathe, but the air in my lungs felt heavy, like steam, and the crimson magic smelled faintly metallic in my nostrils. A tingling sensation began on my upper lip, where a bit of blood had dried, and zinged up my nose.

The sensation was too intense, and I sneezed. When I opened my eyes, the crimson magic was gone. But the tingle remained, zinging around in my sinuses as if the magic were still reacting with my blood.

I blinked at the windshield, still focused on the sensations and not really seeing anything beyond the glass.

I felt vital. Energized. Almost as if I'd gone back for more healing. My adrenaline had faded, and my anger had died down to an ache in my chest.

It wasn't that I was okay with what Zarella had said, but I was calmer. Focused. Thoughts were becoming clearer, and as I sat there in my truck in the freezing cold, something dawned on me. Zarella had kept me in a position of weakness, stringing me along and chastising me. But I wasn't weak. I carried more magics in me than most crafters would dream of, and I was as powerful as any Level III alive. My biggest problem was that I was unskilled. Well, that was too damn bad. I didn't have years to train. But I had plenty of tricks up my sleeve, and I was suddenly sure that if I could figure out how to use the blood-red magic, it would be the crucial thing I needed to take on Damien and the Steins.

I reached for the key in the ignition, started the engine, and then flipped a U-turn and headed home.

Loki greeted me in the dark apartment. After setting my keys on the table near the door, I dropped to one knee and took his face in my hands so I could scratch behind his ears. Faint fiery light flickered deep in his irises as he panted happily at the attention.

"Good boy," I whispered, giving his head one final pat before rising. "Want some kibble?"

He followed me to the kitchen, where I used his bowl to scoop out a generous portion of dog food. Leaving him to chomp his way through it, I went to the living room and stretched out on the sofa with my phone. I was drained past the point of exhaustion, but it would be a while before my brain was ready to shut down for the day.

I scrolled through my emails, stopping when I got one from the Society of the Underworld. I sat up a little straighter. With everything else going on, I'd nearly forgotten the Society had a meeting scheduled for the next night. It would be only my third since getting inducted into the group. The memory sent a sharp pang through my heart. Rogan had been there for the first one. He'd introduced me around. And after, he and I had spent the night together for the first time. It wasn't long after that he'd become possessed by a genetically modified demon and then had killed a Supernatural Forces soldier, thereby rendering himself unsalvageable. Once a possessed person killed, the demon can't be exorcised. The only safe option is euthanizing with obliteration magic.

I pressed my lips together and pulled them in between my teeth, biting down hard to keep tears from springing to my eyes. Deep down, I'd probably known that Rogan and I couldn't last. After all, he hadn't truly belonged in the realm of the living. But still, the loss hurt.

Zarella was part of the Society, actually one of the more powerful members, but Rogan had been a member for longer than Zarella. I'd always thought Rogan was a hermit with no real social ties, but since his Earthly death and return to the *in-between*, I'd learned he did have a few friends in the Society. Perhaps they'd know something about the crimson magic and be willing to keep it secret. I'd start with Florica, the Romani woman who served as the secretary for the Society.

With that intention set, my mind seemed ready to let go, and consciousness faded into sleep.

While Deb was at work the next day, I alternately scoured supernatural contract job listings and tried to learn more about the Steins.

I knew Damien's family was essentially mage royalty, but the mages were extremely secretive. In fact, they'd only revealed themselves to the world after the Manhattan Rip because they'd felt obligated to come forward and offer their powers to help stem the tide of demons pouring through into our world. Since then, they'd managed to avoid the media to an admirable extent.

I'd actually seen Damien's parents in person not long ago, when I'd been briefly held prisoner on the Gregori Industries campus. His mother and father were beautiful, imposing, and cold. They'd come to take Evan from my uncle Jacob Gregori, which he had clearly not been happy about. But Damien had helped me escape and break Evan free. I'd thought my former partner had good intentions, but he'd stolen Evan from me within hours. Until the confrontation in San Francisco, that had been the last time I'd seen either of them.

My thoughts suddenly flicked to a different track, the one that cropped up every once in a while and repeatedly told me I was an idiot when it came to men. Damien wasn't even a romantic interest—he was gay—and yet it seemed I'd still been naïve about what he really valued. The past several years had been a string of misjudgments about men, starting with getting into a relationship with Brady Chancellor, a Strike Team guy who I much later realized was actually kind of an asshole. Johnny Beemer had been a slight improvement, in that he was a decent guy for the most part, but we were a bad match. With Rogan, I'd briefly felt at home, but he was a reaper trapped in a man's body, and the whole thing was probably doomed from the start.

Deb came in the door, her winter jacket straining over the roundness of her belly. The coat was second-hand, one we'd found a couple weeks ago after she could no longer close the zipper on the one she usually wore.

Her brows shot up as she took in my expression. "You look pensive. Everything okay?"

I sighed and rubbed one hand across my forehead. "Yeah, just thinking of Rogan. And men in general."

"Uh oh."

She put her school bag and purse down on the leather chair and began unwinding the plaid scarf around her neck.

It clashed terribly with the pink coat, but we didn't have the luxury of being picky.

"I think I might be getting a little better," I said. "Rogan was the best one yet. Except for, you know, the not-being-totally-human part. And his death wish. Okay, maybe I haven't improved all that much."

She gave me a little sympathetic tilt of her head.

"I might go on a date this weekend," I blurted.

Her eyes widened. "With who?"

"Caleb Montgomery. We've run into each other a couple of times on jobs."

"He's not another Johnny Beemer, is he?"

I shook my head. "No, he seems very down to Earth. He's new here, part of the Supernatural Forces special team." I held up a hand. "I know what you're thinking, but he's nothing like Brady. That I can see so far, anyway. Hey, you should meet him. I need your take. I don't completely trust myself."

"Of course I'd love to meet him!" She gave a rueful laugh. "I'm not sure I'm a great judge of men, though."

"Maybe not always with yourself, but I think that's pretty normal. You've always given me great advice. In fact, it probably would have been better if you'd been a hell of a lot more heavy-handed with it." I echoed her laugh.

"Tell him to come here to pick you up, and we'll invite him in for a beer," she said. "And you know, there's nothing wrong with taking things slowly. Taking some time to really try to see someone clearly . . ."

She'd trailed off in a way that made me think she was talking partly to herself.

"How's *Chris*?" I said, loading Lagatuda's name with importance.

Deb tried to scowl at me, but she was too cute to put any real menace behind it. "We're talking about you, not me."

I arched a brow. "Are we? Kind of sounded like you were talking about yourself, too."

"Well, *Chris* is *fine*."

She turned away, but not before I saw her cheeks pinking and a little smile playing over her lips.

"Good," I said. "Be sure to tell him hi next time he texts."

"If he does, I will."

I chuckled to myself. She disappeared into the bedroom to change out of her school teacher clothes, as was her ritual these days when she got home. She'd turned into a bit of a cat in recent weeks, curling up in sweats under a blanket with a cup of herbal tea nearby. I was just glad the pregnancy was going well, and she seemed relatively happy considering all the stress in her life. Not long ago, the very thought of having a roommate made me shudder. But I'd grown to love having Deb around and didn't really want to think of things changing.

"Want soup for dinner?" Deb asked, reemerging from the bedroom in her favorite purple sweatpants and a gray men's pullover sweatshirt we'd found on a clearance rack at Walmart.

"Nah, I'm good," I said, closing my laptop. I stood and stretched. "I'm exhausted."

I slept hard and must have turned off my alarm because Deb was long gone by the time I woke up. She came home in the evening with a grocery bag in one hand.

"I know I shouldn't have spent the money, but I was just really craving steak," she said. "Split it with me?"

"Thanks for the offer, but you enjoy it," I said. "I've gotta take off anyway. There's a Society meeting tonight."

Apprehension flickered across her face. She wasn't crazy about my involvement with the Underworld. It was a lot different than the coven, granted, but Society meetings didn't involve any sacrifices or spooky dealings. Well, except for the zombie proxies that some of the remote members sent to attend in their place. So that was a little weird. But otherwise, it was mostly an excuse to get together and drink home-distilled vodka in the mancave of a local wealthy car dealership owner who also happened to be a necromancer.

"Do you want me to drop you?" she asked. "I don't like the idea of you driving back late after drinking."

Loki stood and stretched, too, and perked up as he watched me. He'd developed a sense for when I was going to leave the house, and these days he came with me most of the time.

"I promise I'll only have one drink," I said. "You know I'd get a ride with someone or order a cab if I weren't fit to drive."

We both knew we didn't have money to spare for a cab.

"Just please be careful," she said.

"I'll be fine, Deb, promise. Enjoy the steak." I gestured toward the kitchen. "I got some of that Greek yogurt you like today, too."

The tension eased from her face, replaced by an appreciative smile. "I'll have some for dessert. Thanks."

I gave her a little wave, scooped up my keys, and then Loki and I were out the door. He jumped in and sat on the passenger seat, panting with a doggy smile on his face. I'd taken him to Ed's last Society meeting, and everyone had fawned over the hellhound-doodle and insisted I bring Loki again.

I was actually looking forward to the get-together. I felt more at home among the hard-drinking necromancers than I did with the coven witches. Plus, I was hoping to find answers to my questions about the blood-red magic.

E𝐷 Jensen lived in a mansion at the end of a private road off the highway that led to the local ski hill. As I left Boise behind and made my way up in elevation, I began to relax a little. Ed's place was only about ten miles from the heart of downtown, but it felt more remote than that, surrounded by conifers and silence. The darkness of nature took over, without city lights to interfere with the night.

When I pulled up to the house, there were already a few cars parked along the edges of the driveway. Ed was the perennial host of the regional Society meetings, and his strange, giant house was somehow perfect for gatherings of Underworlders. The outside looked like a refurbished Egyptian ruin, with sloped sides and deep doorways flanked by lit torches.

I let myself in through the front door, and Loki and I navigated the dim hallways, lit with occasional wall sconces that held actual live flames. Ed was a fantasy buff, and the murals on the walls depicted scenes from stories and games.

As I neared the man cave that was part pool hall and part theater, muted conversation and the sound of a game on the TV drifted toward me. When I entered, I was greeted with waves from the group gathered at the bar. Mark, the unassuming guy who looked like a junior high math teacher, was pouring drinks. He was actually the leader of the Society, though you never would have guessed it by looking at him. When he caught sight of me, he grabbed a frosty beer mug from under the counter, pulled the tap of a local lager, filled the glass, and then slid the foaming glass down to meet my hand just as I joined the milling Underworlders.

Florica bent to fawn over Loki, ruffling his ears and speaking to him affectionately in her native language.

I'd thought I'd arrived quite early, and I was surprised so many others were already there. I peered around at everyone.

"What's going on?" I asked Ed, who was holding a cocktail. "Everyone seems kind of quiet."

His usually jocular face was drawn. He and Mark traded a look. Then Ed tipped his head toward a TV at the other end of the room that was showing sports scores on mute. Two men sat on a leather sofa under the TV, and they looked deep in conversation.

One of the men looked up, and his eyes locked on mine at the same moment I recognized him. I sucked in a sharp breath, choking a little as my blood ran cold.

"How . . . ? What the hell is Phillip Zarella doing here?" I asked Ed.

I flipped my gaze back to the men on the sofa, trying to make sure I wasn't seeing things.

"He's out," Mark said quietly.

I stared incredulously back and forth between him and Ed. "Out? What does that mean?"

Mark shrugged. "He's no longer confined to the Gregori campus, apparently."

I blinked several times as my stomach began to knot. "I don't understand."

Florica straightened. "Rumor is that he supplied information to the government," she said in her thick accent. "And in return he will not be re-arrested as long as he stays out of the media and out of trouble."

"That's insane," I hissed, trying my best not to allow my voice to rise. "What could he possibly have handed over?"

Mark shrugged and shook his head. "No one knows yet."

But my hand clenched convulsively around my cold mug as I remembered something. Damien had become a mage by doing a favor for Zarella. My former partner had retrieved a small box and presumably passed the contents to the madman. I'd found the empty box in Damien's apartment later but never knew what had been inside. At first I'd suspected it might be a magical object of great power, but later I began to think it might have been information. Whatever it was, it must have been the bargaining chip Zarella had used to gain his freedom.

I felt sick. Sure, I'd been collaborating with Zarella in the interest of freeing Evan, but allowing Zarella to go *free*? Hell no.

Phillip Zarella had been convicted of horrendous crimes against humanity. He'd been living on the East Coast, not far from the original Gregori Industries, back in a time when laws hadn't caught up with advances in magical technology. Zarella had taken full advantage of the situation, doing experiments on volunteers, most of whom were from severely disadvantaged segments of society. His lab had been located in an area frequented by drug addicts, hookers, and others on the fringes, and there had been "accidental" releases of magitech into nearby areas. He'd also preyed on people desperate for cures to terminal diseases. By the time his work gained enough exposure for him to be investigated and then arrested, his experiments had already affected thousands. The evil genius was like something out of a comic book.

Ed turned away to greet someone else, and Florica drifted over to where she'd set down her drink.

"But . . ." I turned to Mark, baffled. "We just let him be here?"

"I know, it's unsavory to many of us," Mark said quietly. He winced. "That was a gross understatement. But he's a member, and a powerful one at that. Good or bad, he's one of us."

I took a swig of beer to help push down the bile that was trying to rise up my throat. Mark's comment reminded me of something Rogan had said. That Underworlders were like any other slice of society—a mix of good, bad, flawed, and real people. There was a segment of the Society that was like Zarella. They thrived on dark chaos.

I eyed him, and he lifted a hand in a small wave. My mouth twisted with distaste. I couldn't believe he was *there*. He belonged behind bars. Actually, he didn't even deserve that.

It made me feel even more nauseated that I'd been in frequent contact with him lately. And what had it gotten me? My brother was still in Damien's hands.

I intercepted Florica as she moved away from the bar.

"I was wondering if you might be able to help me with something," I said.

"I will try, of course," she said with a genuine smile.

"Do you know anything about maroon magic the color of blood?" I asked. "It's associated with death, I think."

I tried not to think of the fact that there was one person who probably had some knowledge about this magic or would know how to dig it up. Damien. He was obsessed with such knowledge, always entering neatly printed entries into his notebooks. He'd studied advanced magics in college and probably knew as much as any so-called expert in the world.

Florica was a different sort of expert. She collected the lore of her people, recording tales that had been passed down through the Romani for many generations. I'd briefly spoken with her about it at the last meeting, and it sounded like she'd already amassed an incredibly rich store of information. She considered herself a cultural historian of sorts.

Florica pursed her lips and drew a long breath before speaking. "Is this the magic that is sometimes left behind by those who walk in both realms? Trailings?" She fluttered her fingers low behind her, indicating the floor at her heels. Her heavy metal bracelets clinked softly on her wrist.

I blinked, and it took me a second to understand what she meant. "Oh, trails! Yes, that's the stuff. Do you have any experience with it?"

"Not directly, of course, as I do not pass between realms." Her gaze sharpened on me. "But you have this magic, yes?"

I licked my dry lips. "I don't want anyone to know. Can you keep it secret?"

"My people, we are bred for secrecy," she said, her eyes gleaming and her accent thickening. "For centuries, our secrets were the only things that kept us alive."

I inclined my head in an acknowledgment of her history.

"Besides," she said. "I like, you, Ella. You're strange like me. But, thank God, not strange like . . ." She raised her chin toward the end of the room where Zarella still sat.

More members had arrived, and everyone was taking note of Zarella's presence. There was a foreign sort of tension in the air, an uneasiness hanging over the usually jocular group. It was one thing to have Zarella attending by proxy, commanding a zombie to use as his ears, eyes, and voice, but quite another to have the madman himself lounging on one of Ed's couches.

I gave Florica a mock-bashful look. "Why, thank you for the compliment."

She chuckled. "Now. This crimson magic. The color is no accident. My people call it blood magic. The trailings have no power. They are like footprints or the slime left by a, how you say, snail? But it can be commanded. From what I remember, it works only in the presence of blood. But not just blood, simply there. The blood must be fresh from a sacrifice."

I frowned. Sacrifice? That didn't jibe with my experience. The crimson red magic had come forth, surrounding my hands, when I'd gotten angry. Oh. But there *had* been blood involved. Mine, leaking from my nose when I pushed my magic too hard.

"Are there any other ways it can be wielded?" I asked.

"It is known in my people's lore as blood sacrifice magic. In other cultures, it is known as plague magic, but I do not know precisely what that means," she said. Her eyes narrowed as she took in my confusion. "But you have different knowledge, yes?"

"I think so," I said haltingly. "I'm not really sure. I've brought it forth a couple of times, but there was no sacrifice involved. It was rather accidental. I want to learn to use it, though."

I nearly kept talking but instead cut off, snapping my jaw closed with a click, cautious about saying too much. It wasn't that I mistrusted Florica. I just had a sudden, deep certainty that this magic would be my secret weapon when it came time to get Evan back from Damien or the Order of Mages or whoever had him. The silver magic of the *in-between* was powerful, but it was also killing me to use it. The blood magic originated from *this* realm, from my world. It would still harm me if I pushed it too far—any magic could cause exhaustion and even irreversible brain damage or death if pushed to the extreme—but it wasn't foreign.

"It is very rare," Florica said. "And I doubt there is much recorded information about it. I don't know anything more."

"Thank you, all the same. And I do appreciate your discretion."

She gave me an odd, stiff smile and sidled away rather rapidly. When I turned, I found out why. Zarella was standing there, obviously waiting to talk to me.

"Ella," he said. "We've had so few opportunities to speak in person. This is rather a treat."

Everything in me was screaming to back away, that to even be in such proximity of the man was abhorrent, as if his crimes hung in the air like an oily residue and might settle on me. But I sipped my beer, trying not to flit my gaze around as others took notice of the two of us.

"I thought you were finished with me," I said coldly.

His brows rose, and he gave me a hurt look. "Can't I simply say hello?"

"No," I said. I set my empty bottle on the bar and walked away.

He'd jerked me around enough. And the whole time, I'd felt sick at the idea of any involvement with him. I'd buried the feelings under my desperation to save Evan. But now, I desperately wished for a way to do it without Zarella.

An itchy sort of impatience flooded through me. I looked around, thinking I might just slip out and leave, but Mark was calling the meeting to order, and I'd already put myself too far into the middle of the room. If I walked out, everyone would see me leave.

I stuck close to Florica, taking comfort in the sense that she was somewhat of an ally, and tried to make myself inconspicuous at the edge of the group. The Society members had formed a loose crowd near one of the pool tables, some of them leaning against it and others taking seats in the nearby rows of home-theater chairs.

Florica went forward to read minutes from the last meeting. There wasn't a ton to say, as the last time we'd gathered it was near Christmas and the Society had paused most activities for the holidays. I mostly tuned out as Mark took over again, talking about possible activities and commitments for the coming year, and instead considered everything I had at my disposal.

More than anything, I wished Rogan were still there. I bit down hard on my lower lip, the physical pain distracting me from a sudden wave of sorrow. Rogan was gone, but he'd left me with a great gift. The knowledge of how to use water in the *in-between* to move long distances instantly and undetected. He'd also introduced me to Switchboard, a reclusive mage living in the mountains of Idaho.

It would be very useful to have a mage on my side. But I wasn't sure if I could convince Switch to help me. He was a strange old guy who obviously didn't care much for the rest of humanity, but perhaps I could persuade him. It was worth a try.

My mind spun as I thought of everything I needed to do. Find Evan's new location. Gather my resources. Talk to Switch. Get ready to face Damien and the mages.

And the blood magic was still gnawing at me—I had to learn what I could do with it.

My eyes flicked to Zarella. He also stood at the edge of the group, a bit apart, in a spot that seemed somehow cast in shadow. He didn't need to know that I wanted to strike out on my own. In fact, I might be able to find a way to use him, to take the upper hand with Zarella.

Could I fool the madman? I wouldn't know until I tried.

After leaving Ed's, I stayed up nearly all night, hunched over my laptop doing research. I decided to try to pretend that I was Damien and learn all I could about the blood magic. It was rare, which would give me an edge against powerful crafters like the mages, especially if they didn't know I possessed it. Where would Damien go for information about a strange, rare magic?

He'd been a scholar his entire life, taking classes, earning degrees, learning skills, conducting research, and training in various magics and weapons. I didn't have time to be that thorough, but I figured I might be able to make use of some of his resources and tactics. I looked up the universities he'd attended to earn his degrees in magical studies. Surely those places had extensive resources.

I found a website with a database of scholarly papers on the topics of magic, magical technology, and similar topics. I really wished I knew someone in academia, but most of the people I associated with were blue-collar folks who never had the money for high-priced degrees.

When the bedroom door opened and Deb emerged, she and I both jumped a little.

"Is it morning?" I asked incredulously.

At the same time, she said, "What are you doing up?"

"My alarm just went off," she said.

I tilted my head, cracking my neck, as I realized how stiff I was. "I guess I stayed up all night."

"Doing what?"

"Research," I said. "Hey, do you know anyone with access to university research libraries."

She spread her arms in a ta-da motion. "Um, me?"

I tilted my head skyward. Of course. Deb took one class a year through Boise State University's online program, as she slowly made her way through another advanced certification. She wanted to work with special needs kids eventually, so she was earning the necessary credentials.

"Is there any possibility that BSU's library connects to other libraries?"

"Yep. Whatcha need?"

"Some magical research," I said. "Academic papers."

She came over to my laptop, opened a new browser window, and went to BSU's student portal, where she entered her credentials.

"Just use my account and order whatever papers you need," she said. "Most of them should be available immediately for download if they're through other libraries."

I reached up to hug her waist with one arm. "Thank you, this is perfect."

She giggled. "I've never seen you get excited about anything to do with school or research. What are you looking up?"

"Trying to find anything I can about my magic," I said, staying purposely vague about the blood magic. "I figure if I can give myself a quick crash course, it can't hurt, right?"

Deb's expression sobered. "I really wish you wouldn't go after Damien alone, Ella." She looked conflicted. "I understand you have to do anything you can for your brother, but . . . I don't see how you stand a chance against a mage. I just don't want you to end up dead."

"I know." I sucked in a heavy breath and then thumped the center of my chest. "My reaper makes me very, very difficult to kill, don't forget that. Believe me, I don't want to end up dead, either. I've waited a very long time to find Evan."

She gave me a sad little smile and went into the kitchen. She emerged a few minutes later with a mug of tea, which she took into the bathroom with her. A moment later, the water in the shower turned on.

I scrubbed my hands down my face as my sleepless night started to catch up with me. But I pushed on, doing searches through Deb's account and refining my terms a little each time.

Deb left for school, and some time after that I started to nod off over the keyboard. I came to with a start and gave my head a shake.

Loki, who'd been dozing next to me on the sofa, looked up expectantly.

"Ughhh," I moaned. "I can't just sit here reading papers. We've gotta talk to Switch. And find out what Damien's done with Evan."

My body wanted me to lie down and take a nap, but my mind was whirling. I jumped in the shower, and that woke me up a little. Then I brewed a very strong pot of coffee and filled an insulated gas station travel tumbler with the dark, steaming liquid. Then I groaned.

"Well, shit." I looked down at the mug and then over at Loki. "This won't travel the way we're going."

I plugged the kitchen sink and turned on the water, and with the mug in my hand, I went to get my warmest winter jacket. I took a few gulps, scalding my tongue, as I waited for a couple inches of water to fill the bottom of the sink. Then I shut off the water, set the mug on the counter, gave it one last longing look, and let myself fade into the *in-between*. My hellhound-doodle joined me. I took a moment to picture the road leading to Switchboard's cabin in the mountains, specifically the little stream next to the road, conjuring it as exactly as I could from memory, and then used Rogan's trick to take us there.

We transported to an isolated spot in the mountains that would have taken me about three hours to reach in my truck. The ghostly shape of the old car up on cinderblocks told me I was in the right spot.

Following the tug of the living realm, I found myself standing in a thickly-wooded area with patches of snow still over a foot deep under the trees. The path leading to Switch's cabin had been tramped down until the snow was a compact, dirty layer that had frozen to a crust on the top.

The memory of being there with Rogan punched through me, and I paused for a second to collect myself.

My breath puffed in pale white clouds, and the cold was already stinging my cheeks. Loki had bounded several yards ahead but stopped and turned to wait for me. I just hoped Switch didn't get twitchy with one of his shotguns and accidentally shoot my sweet dog. Unlikely, seeing as how the hermit mage was a telepath. He should have sensed us—or me, at least—the moment we arrived in the vicinity. Still, I moved slowly, not wanting to cause him alarm.

The air was cold and crisp enough to make my nasal passages tingle and my eyes water. Last time, with Rogan, there'd been the barest dusting of snowfall but no accumulation of the stuff yet. It barely looked like the same place now, with the conifer boughs weighed down by snow and the ground mostly obscured.

Loki was waiting for me at the door by the time I was close enough to the cabin to see movement behind one window. Switch was home, and that was lucky for me. Rogan had said that Switch sometimes went out hunting for days at a time. I couldn't imagine doing that this time of year, but the hermit mage was obviously accustomed to a very rustic life. He probably thought nothing of it. Probably didn't even need a proper shelter.

The door creaked open as I approached.

"What happened to yer magic?" Switch croaked at me. His voice crackled around the edges, as if he hadn't spoken at full volume in quite some time.

I raised a hand in greeting. "Hi, Switchboard. I'm a Level III now."

"Obviously. How'd ya manage that?" He swung the door wide. "Git inside, woman, before all the heat escapes."

I scooted through the doorway. Loki went over to the dirty rag rug in front of the fire, circled a few times, and then plopped down with a contented sigh.

"Damien Stein did it," I said.

I glanced around the one-room abode. It hadn't changed much. Logs burned in the fireplace, dirty dishes filled the wash basin, and the bed was rumpled. Switch himself looked about the same, too—like a caricature of an old-timey miner, with weathered skin, a long scraggly beard, and suspenders over a grimy shirt.

"Ack," Switch scoffed. He hocked a wad of tobacco juice into the tin cup he held in one hand. "Went and made himself a mage, I heard. Shouldn't mess with the natural way of things. Where's the reaper man?"

For a second, I wasn't sure who he was talking about.

"Rogan died," I said quietly. "Well, he's not gone, exactly. He passed back to the *in-between*."

Switch grunted and nodded, seeming to mull that over. "Good for him, I suppose."

I shrugged. "It was what he wanted, so yeah."

"Whatcha want from old Switchboard, girlie? It ain't the pleasure of my company, I'm guessin'." He gave a dry cackle-cough.

He seemed to be in a decent mood. I took a breath. I figured I might as well go for broke and make the biggest ask first.

"I need help," I said. "Damien Stein took my brother, Evan. Damien intends to give him to the mages, if he hasn't already. They will use Evan to try to permanently close the rips, but it would mean my brother's death. Evan is innocent, and he doesn't deserve to be a pawn in the mage's schemes. I'm not going to let anyone use my brother as a sacrificial lamb. There has to be another way. I've come to ask you to go with me to face the mages and save my brother."

He'd gone over to perch near the fire on one of the seats there—a cut log tipped on its end to provide a rustic chair.

He propped one fist on his hip and regarded me with his pale gray-blue. Galaxies swirled in his irises.

"Passionate speech," Switch said.

I waited for him to say more. When a few seconds of silence ticked by, I shifted my weight.

"So, will you go?" I asked.

He barked a laugh. "God, no. I'm done with those bastards and their Order. Rips or no rips, I don't give a dang." He spit into his cup again.

My face tightened. "It's not about the rips, or the mages. It's about an innocent, troubled person who will be murdered at the hands of people who should have prevented the disaster in the first place."

"Yer brother, yep. By all accounts, he is the one who can seal it all up."

The back of my neck heated as agitation prickled through me. "You think it's fine, then, to kill someone to atone for sins he didn't commit? You think murder is justified?"

He waved a hand. "Justified or not, it ain't my business."

"Why? Because you can just carry on out here in the wilderness regardless? Because it doesn't affect you?" My voice strained as I tried to keep it under control.

But my hands were shaking with pent-up anger. Why was everyone so damn *fine* with murdering my brother? So casual about ending the life of someone who'd never even had a chance at a normal existence in his nearly twenty years?

"Because I chose long ago to break with the mages," he said. "And the only reason I'm still here is that I've kept to myself."

"Fine," I said, my patience thinned down to nothing. "Hope you enjoy your self-preservation."

I turned on my heel and was poised with my hand on the door when the air in the room changed. The crackle of magic at my back, like an electric wind, made me turn.

There, in the middle of Switchboard's one-room cabin, a thin, black vertical line loomed nearly floor to ceiling. It widened like a giant slit of a cat's pupil in the dark, and neon blue wisps of magic licked out around the edges.

My breath stilled as the rip grew to fill half the cabin. Something glimmered beyond it, many-colored twinkles like fairy lights. Hot air buffeted toward me, blowing back my hair, and the scent of sulfurous flame filled my nose. Loki came to stand at my side, his hackles up.

"Don't you want to see what else I might have to offer you?" a voice from within asked.

I caught a glimpse of sparkling crystals and knew exactly what awaited me. I swallowed hard and strode toward the tear between dimensions. It was only when I stood right at the edge of the rip that I realized Switch was no longer in the cabin.

Pulling my arms in against my sides and ducking my head, I stepped through the rip.

As soon as I stepped into the enormous cavern, I knew exactly where I was: the crystal cave where I'd met the dragon oracle.

The dragon itself hadn't fully materialized yet, but the rip through which it would emerge had already formed. I licked my dry lips and glanced around at the thousands of glittering crystals that decorated the walls and ceiling. Just like standing in the middle of a geode, with each pointed gem lit from within. Before, I'd been filled with wonder at the sight, but now it struck me just how horribly all those points could tear a person up. Like thousands of pretty knives just waiting to rip flesh.

Loki had come through with me, and hellfire danced bright and orange in his eyes. He seemed excited, and when his coat darkened and grew bristly, I knew he was on the verge of transforming into his huge, black hellhound form.

I squinted into the dark void of the rip that was opening up ahead. I sensed a large form on the other side and thought I saw the darker silhouette of the huge beast.

"Ella Grey," the voice of the dragon intoned, so deep the ground vibrated a little.

"Uh, yes," I said. "Hi. I'm not sure how—"

"How you came to be here in my presence?" the dragon interrupted.

"Yeah."

I held my breath as the creature stepped through like some great winged dinosaur. I recalled the other times I'd stood before the oracle and suddenly remembered something.

Shit.

I had no offering. The oracle liked sparkly trinkets, but I didn't have anything to give. It wasn't my fault I'd shown up empty-handed. I hadn't expected to be there. But the dragon could be cranky, and probably wouldn't be interested in excuses. I'd just have to hope he didn't demand a gift.

"You don't recognize me?" the creature asked. It turned its serpentine head to the side to peer at me with one eye and snorted hot steam through its nostrils.

I squinted up at it in confusion.

"Yeah of course I do. I mean, we've met before," I stammered. "You're pretty hard to forget."

Then the beast let out a cackle of a laugh, and something about it . . .

My eyes slowly widened. "Are you . . . Switch?"

The dragon made a little tee-hee, and some sulfurous sparks shot from its nose. "You really didn't know before?"

I shook my head vehemently. "I had no idea."

I couldn't really even fathom what it meant. Was he using some sort of super-powered illusion magic? Was he actually part beast?

"This is why I can't interfere," it said. *He*—not it. That was Switch in there, hard as it was to believe. "Oracles may only be consulted about the moves; they may not participate in the game."

Game? I tried to brush off the implication that my brother's life was just part of some grand amusement.

"You may ask a question," he said with a magnanimous air.

I didn't need sessions with oracles. I needed power. What I *needed* was a fricking mage on my side. Even better, an army of them. But this was what he was offering, and he seemed to think it might be useful to me.

I took in a slow breath and closed my eyes briefly, pushing away my irritation and focusing on the opportunity that was being presented. The image of Evan's face floated through my mind's eye. Not the emaciated drug addict he'd become, but the way he looked when he was a child. His laughing eyes on his eighth birthday when we'd rented a hotel room for a night in the middle of winter so he could swim in a heated pool. It was a huge luxury, and my mother, grandmother, and I had scraped money together for months to make it happen. But watching him splash and swim, it'd been worth the sacrifice. He'd had the capacity for happiness, once.

I opened my eyes and faced the dragon. "What do I need to know or understand in order to keep my brother from being murdered by the mages, Jacob Gregori, or anyone else who might want to sacrifice him to close the rips?" I asked.

I braced myself for an outburst. The oracle didn't like it if you asked the "wrong" question. But the anger didn't come. Perhaps I was getting better at this.

"I have three responses to give you, Ella Grey." The dragon paused, it seemed, for dramatic effect. It worked. I stood there holding my breath. "One, you can't do this alone. You and your hellhound aren't enough. Two, you'll need an adversary to become an ally, or you don't stand a chance. And three, the demonic rips must be closed. It's time. But someone *will* die to accomplish this end."

As he'd spoken, his head had moved slowly down and forward toward me, weaving slightly back and forth like a snake's. His words seemed to echo around in the cavern as the dragon and I faced each other, his huge snout only a few feet from my face.

Gold flakes crusted the creature's scales, giving him a metallic shimmer, and fire blazed in his eyes. I wondered how long Switchboard had been a dragon, and if there were others like him. Whether he'd been born an oracle or had come into it later in life. How many people had stood before him, seeking answers. How many he'd killed in a fiery rage.

But none of that was important. Switchboard had given me all he was willing to give. I had to move on.

"Godspeed, Ella Grey," the oracle whispered to me.

The whoosh of a sudden wind from behind blew my hair forward around my face. I pushed it away and whirled around to find a rip forming. My exit. When I looked back over my shoulder, the oracle was retreating through his own rip.

Loki trotted ahead of me and gracefully leaped through the opening. He hadn't gone full hellhound, and I was grateful. I didn't believe he would hurt me, but it made me jumpy to see him as a giant black dog with fiery eyes and brimstone breath.

We got dumped back out into Switchboard's cabin. The fire still crackled in the hearth, and everything else looked the same. Switch wasn't there, and somehow I knew he wouldn't show up again while we remained. He wasn't much of a host.

"C'mon boy," I said. "Let's get back home and figure out what's next."

I went to the sink and pulled out the cleanest of the bowls piled there. Working the pump handle faucet, I managed to fill it with a couple inches of water. Loki and I faded to the *in-between* and then home to the kitchen, where I always left a bowl of water on the counter to use for this purpose, just in case the water in the sink drained while I was away.

Back in the apartment, I made a sandwich to quiet my growling stomach, and while I ate, I flipped through the research papers I'd downloaded.

One of them was titled "Magics Utilizing Bodily Fluids for Activation: An Etiological Study." I had no idea what "etiological" meant, but the bodily fluids part snagged my attention because Florica had said the crimson magic was related to blood sacrifice, and because of Jen's reaction when I'd accidentally summoned the magic during the coven meeting.

I began wading through the paper. There was a part about bloodletting. When I got to the discussion about the proposed mechanism of spontaneous healing that had been observed when bloodletting was combined with certain magics, I knew I was on the right track.

I opened a blank document on my laptop and started making notes. When I got to the end of the paper, I looked up the researcher's name—Esmerelda Aguilar—and downloaded three more papers she'd written. As I scanned through them, I felt a sudden pang of longing. I wished I could share my newfound academic excitement with the one person who would have really appreciated it: Damien.

My enthusiasm faded a little as I recalled the oracle's warnings. I couldn't succeed alone, and I needed an adversary to turn ally. Damien was an adversary, but I had a feeling he wasn't the one the dragon had been talking about. He was too far gone and too deeply invested in trying to heal his own lifelong wounds.

Phillip Zarella, perhaps? Or maybe my uncle Jacob. Either of those options made me squirm—I wanted nothing to do with either man. I'd intended to try to use Zarella, but maybe that was the wrong tactic.

I squeezed my eyes closed and rubbed my forehead.

A knock at the door pulled me out of my thoughts.

Loki was wagging his tail before I even opened door.

"Roxanne?" I said, surprised to see the blond teenager standing on the porch. I'd met her several months ago, when I'd helped her get her brother out of a jam. Ever since, she'd been a sort of unofficial little sister to the coven, and Deb had been mentoring her in magic.

"Nathan had to take a job on a fishing boat for a while," she said. She came in and unceremoniously dumped her overstuffed, frayed backpack on the floor. "We gave up the apartment. Deb said I could stay here."

I just stared at her for a second.

"Uh, yeah, sure," I said finally, alternately impressed and a little concerned about how unconcerned Roxanne seemed about the whole thing and also wracking my memory.

Had Deb mentioned Roxanne moving in and I just forgot? I looked around the tiny apartment with a sinking feeling.

I was already sleeping on the sofa. We were going to have to try to borrow a camping cot or something for Roxanne. I couldn't even think about what it would be like when I brought my brother home. And then Deb's baby arrived. Three adults, two kids, and a hellhound-doodle in here? I pulled a hand down my face but then pushed my concerns to the back of my mind. We'd figure it out.

"Shouldn't you be in school?" I asked.

Roxanne had already flopped on the sofa, pulled up her feet, and was intent on her phone in one hand and absently patting Loki's head with the other hand.

She looked up. "School got out, like, a half hour ago."

I checked the time on my phone. "Oh, right."

"Hey, I want to make dinner for you guys," she asked. "Can I do spaghetti?"

I spread my hands in a welcoming gesture. "Absolutely."

That was the thing about Roxanne. She acted like a typical sullen teenage girl some of the time, but then she'd make sweet gestures like fixing dinner, or she'd shout your name across a room, run at you, and throw her skinny arms around your waist in a hug.

"Can I have some money to get spaghetti stuff at the store?" she asked.

My eyes bugged. "Wait, you're not buying?"

"Uhhh . . ."

"Just kidding," I said. "Get whatever else you want, too."

I pulled a few bills out of my pocket and passed them to her. Roxanne was pretty enterprising—from a young age she'd had to find ways to contribute to household income—but I didn't expect her to pay for food while she was staying with us. She was also an expert at how to make meals on a tight budget, which was ideal for Deb's and my current situation. Roxanne knew how to pitch in and understood the concept of pulling your own weight however you could. The thought actually brightened my mood. She was a good kid, and I hadn't seen much of her in the past few weeks. It'd be nice to have her around. I tried to focus on that rather than the extra mouth to feed and the lack of space in the apartment.

"Sweet, thanks," she said, stuffing the money in the kangaroo pocket of her pullover hoodie.

Roxanne put on her parka and headed out to the grocery store that was a couple blocks away, and I powered up my laptop, ready to throw myself back into the research I'd downloaded. Just as I opened one of the documents, my phone rang.

"Hello?" I answered.

"Hi, Ella, this is Becky, your coven sister."

My brows drew together. Becky was the one running against me for Keeper of Means, the treasurer position in the coven. She and I hadn't ever really talked much beyond exchanging pleasantries. She was on the quiet side and hadn't seemed particularly close to anyone in the coven.

"Are you alone?" she asked.

"Uh, yeah, actually."

"Good," she said. "I have some information about the coven's financials that I think might interest you. But I don't want anyone else to know, including Deb."

I closed my laptop. "You've got my attention."

"Am I correct in assuming you don't trust Lynnette?" Becky asked, her tone blunt.

I slid a guilty look off to the side and gave a short, humorless laugh. "Gee, did I not hide that so well?"

She snorted. "Not particularly. I think I can prove that she's cooking the books and lying about a number of things, but I need to get a closer look. Would you be willing to withdraw from the running for Keeper of Means?"

A slow smile began to spread over my face.

"On one condition," I said. "You let me help you take her down."

"I was hoping you'd say that," Becky said. "And actually, I do have something for you."

"Shoot, anything."

"You've got friends at Supernatural Crimes, right?" she asked.

"I've got contacts there, yeah."

"As soon as I get into the financials, I want to double-check all of the freelance jobs she's claimed to have with that organization. I have a feeling there are discrepancies, but I'll need someone there to verify them."

I wasn't sure I could persuade Lagatuda to help me, but I was damn sure willing to try.

"I'll do whatever I can," I said.

"Thanks, Ella," Becky said. She seemed to hesitate over what she wanted to say next. "I know it's going to cause an uproar in the coven if I come forward with this, but I can't just stand by and let her continue to lie."

Relief flooded through me like a cool breeze on a hot day. "You have no idea how glad I am to hear someone else say that," I said.

We hung up a moment later.

I'd been wishing Deb would come to her senses and quit blindly following Lynnette, but that had proved to be an uphill battle. I'd assumed my next best bet was Jen and hoped she might be an ally in trying to take down Lynnette, but I'd never quite been sure I could trust her. Looking back, I realized I should have made a greater effort to get to know the other women and feel out each of them for where they stood in their loyalty to the coven leader. My mood soured a little as I understood my mistake. Just another example of how my anti-social ways had failed me.

The door opened, and I jumped guiltily as Deb walked through.

She peered at me. "Caught you daydreaming?"

"Uh, yeah, I guess I was spacing out," I said.

She spotted Roxanne's things and stopped short, smacking her forehead. "I'm so sorry, I forgot to tell you Rox was coming. My memory is crap lately."

I waved a hand. "No worries. Pregnancy brain."

She gave me a grateful smile and went into the bedroom to put down her things and change.

"She's getting food for dinner," I said.

"Aw, that's nice of her," Deb called from the next room.

My phone pinged with a message, and I half expected it was at text from Becky. But it was an unknown number and the message contained only a Boston address. I frowned. Maybe someone sent it to the wrong number? Then another message came through.

Your brother is there. Go now.

My heart skipped a beat, and then my pulse sped. I stared at my phone for a couple of seconds. Who could it be from? Someone who knew I had the ability to travel long distances very quickly. Damien or Zarella?

I tapped the address to open it in my maps app. I didn't know Boston, but I was going to have to become familiar with a nearby feature so I could visualize it and use the *in-between* to travel there, and I needed to do it fast. With hasty swipes, I zoomed in and looked for anything useful. There, Boston Common, a large urban park, was a handful of blocks from the address. There was a statue of Paul Revere on a horse, and there was a fountain near it. That should do.

I went to the kitchen and began filling the sink with water. While I waited, I studied the photo of the landmark. Loki appeared in the kitchen doorway, watching me. I grabbed his leash out of the drawer. When I turned off the water, he came to sit beside me. We faded into the *in-between* together.

I used the water to take us to Boston Common, a ghostly expanse of paths and blank areas probably filled with grass and other greenery in summer. In the *in-between*, everything was washed-out shades of gray with no signs of life. When we popped back into the land of the living, a little boy of three or four happened to be looking our way while his mother's attention was trained on another lady as the two women chatted. His eyes widened at our sudden appearance and grew even more surprised when he caught sight of Loki. I grinned at the kid and waved. He just stared.

I took out my phone, glanced at the map to orient myself, and then snapped Loki's leash on his collar for the sake of appearances and headed off at a jog for the northwest corner of the park. Boston was overcast, the trees leafless, and the air wintery, slightly warmer but more humid than Boise.

When I arrived half a block down and across the street from a Brownstone building that had been converted into offices, I paused and checked the address again. That was it.

I was just about to cross the street when my phone buzzed in my hand.

Stay out of sight and watch.

I blinked at the message and then looked up and peered around, the hairs on the back of my neck standing up as the creepy sense of being watched washed over me in a shiver. I walked a few steps and then backed into the shadowy nook next to a flight of stairs leading up to a residential Brownstone, taking Loki into the gloom with me. I watched the building across the street. A woman came out and hailed a cab. Another five minutes passed, and nothing happened.

I punched in a reply to the text: *Who are you?*

A moment later a response came: *Someone who just wants to help.*

I squinted at the message as a tiny point of cold apprehension pinged through me. Who would want to help me, besides Zarella? And if it were Zarella, he'd use his code name. He had no reason to stay anonymous with me in these matters. Who was this?

What am I watching for? I texted back.

Nearly a minute went by before I got an answer: *The people who get out of the black cars.*

Just then, three town cars with heavily tinted windows pulled up across the street. I pressed farther into the shadows. One-by-one, the drivers got out and went around to open the back passenger doors.

A stately couple got out of the first car, and my breath caught. It was the Steins, Damien's parents. A second later, Damien himself emerged from the same car. My chest clutched at the sight of my former partner and friend.

When two men emerged from the second car, I stopped breathing. One was my brother. The other was my uncle, Jacob Gregori.

My hand clutched convulsively around my phone, and it took every ounce of my self-control to keep from drawing magic and sprinting across the street to Evan. My chest hitched as I regained breath, and I took a couple of steps forward.

My first urge was to charge, but then the doors of the third car opened, and five people stepped out. I could tell even from a distance that they were mages of the Order. They carried themselves the same way the Steins did—standing rod-straight and looking around at the world as if they not only reigned over it but also stood above it. I backed up again, taking refuge in the shadows.

I watched the group go up the stairs of the Brownstone office building. Damien opened the door and then held it as everyone filed in. Just before he followed them, he flicked a glance left and right, but his gaze skipped right past the place where Loki and I were standing. Damien disappeared inside, and the door drifted closed behind him.

I was no match for eight mages. It would be suicide to try to go up against them. But I couldn't just leave.

Pulling my awareness within, I reached for the realm of my reaper. A moment later, I stood in the gray mist of the *in-between*. Loki and I waited for a gap in the traffic of vehicles that were driverless except for the filmy, nebulous souls of the living that stood in for their corporeal counterparts. Then my dog and I crossed the street and jogged up the steps of the office building.

Once inside, I paused. Which way had they gone? The living weren't visible to me in limbo land. I moved off to the side of the lobby and popped back into the realm of the living just in time to see the last of the mages step onto the elevator. I flattened myself against the wall and waited for the doors to slide closed and then just about plowed into two men in business suits as I hastily scooted over to stare at the numbers illuminating over the elevator. One of them swore when he saw Loki. I ignored the exclamations.

There was a long pause at floor five, but not knowing whether the group had gotten off at that floor or the elevator had stopped to let others on, I had to stay and track the other stops. Five, eight, and fourteen before it began to descend again.

Too impatient to stand there and wait, I went for the stairwell and began sprinting up, taking the stairs two at a time with Loki on my heels.

On the fifth floor, I slipped into the corridor. Some of the office doors were marked with business names, but others had only suite numbers. My heart sank as I realized I'd probably lost the mages.

I slowed to a wandering pace, not sure how to proceed.

"Where'd they go?" I muttered under my breath.

If the mages were close enough, there'd be a little tickle of magical sensation due to the enormous power they were capable of wielding. But my skills were still rudimentary, and I just about had to be staring someone in the face to feel their level of magic. There was no reason to need such close proximity since I'd become a Level III. I just hadn't learned how to stretch out with my senses.

I ground my teeth and let out a frustrated growl. Loki looked up at me, cocking his head.

"Damien?" I asked my hellhound. "Remember him?"

Loki's tongue lolled, and he panted a doggy smile. A woman rounded the corner and let out a squeak when she saw us. She backed up, disappearing from sight, clearly thinking it would be wiser to take a different route. It was probably only a matter of time before someone called security on us.

"Smell his scent anywhere?" I asked Loki, feeling a little ridiculous about expecting him to understand what I was saying.

He turned and began trotting down the hallway. He slowed and began pausing at every object he encountered—a potted plant, a gum wrapper, a pamphlet stand. After a minute or so, it just seemed like he was fiddling. I was just about to turn around and try the lobby to see if there was a receptionist or anyone who might know where a bunch of mages might be meeting, when he stopped at suite 518 and poked his nose at the door. He backed up, sat, and looked at me.

I pointed at the door. "Damien's in there?" I whispered.

His mouth fell open and he panted.

I eyed the door, and then I faded to the *in-between*. Loki joined me.

Damn. The door still stood solid before me. All I wanted was a look at my brother. Just to see if what Damien had said was true, if Evan really was getting clean. If he were in his right mind, he could help in his own escape.

Suddenly Loki began shaking his head and whimpering. I started to bend down to see what was wrong when the door swung inward. Loki disappeared, presumably back into the realm of the living. I nearly followed him but caught myself. If I did, I'd appear right smack in front of whoever had opened the suite's door. Instead, I stayed in limbo land and darted through the open doorway.

Panic gripped me as I realized what I'd done—basically trapped myself in an office full of mages while leaving Loki to fend for himself. If Damien saw my dog, he'd instantly know I was nearby.

But it was too late. The door closed behind me, trapping me inside. The awareness of souls nearby pinged the reaper within. I was more interested in the predicament I'd created. I'd either have to wait until one of the living opened it again so I could escape, or I'd have to leave the *in-between* and take my chances with the mages.

I thought I had those two choices. It turned out I was very, very wrong.

Pressure began to build inside my head. I groaned and then doubled over as it intensified so swiftly I barely keep my balance.

I flailed out one hand as I pitched into the wall. It felt like someone was poking through my ears with pliers and trying to pull my brain out from both sides. I tried to reach for the ley line magic of the *in-between*, but the pain was too great. Then I realized what the pulling sensation was. Something— or someone—was trying to yank me out of limbo land.

With a screech of agony and frustration, I lost my hold on the *in-between*. Back in the land of the living, I fell to my knees, panting and fighting to keep from passing out.

Sensing several sets of eyes on me, I raised my head, squinting through the pain.

The mages had been waiting for me.

Pain pulsed through my head as I looked up at the mages. Damien was there, staring at me with hard detachment as if we'd never been friends. But where was Evan?

I tried to rise, and Damien's mother made a flicking motion with her fingers. Pure white sparks of magic sprayed at me like drops of water. They hit my skin, and every muscle seized with agony. I fell over, my face still turned so I could look up at the mages.

Through the pain, I sensed that one of them—a blond, chisel-featured guy who must have been Damien's brother— had some sort of death magic. A necromancer, maybe. He must have been the one who'd torn me out of the *in-between*. I didn't even know it was possible to do that.

Damien's mother—Sheila was her name, I remembered— twisted her wrist as if turning an invisible doorknob. The pain eased by half.

I sat up, breathing hard, and leaned against the wall for support.

"Where's my brother?" I rasped. My head was swimming, and I was having a hard time keeping a train of thought.

Sheila folded her arms, and a grim smile stretched her lips, which wore the perfect shade of red. A bit dark so as not to be tacky, but intense enough to make her appear effortlessly polished. I bet she never had smudges of it on her teeth. The lipstick wouldn't dare offend her.

Focus. I cursed myself silently.

Sheila's gaze jumped from my eyes to the center of my face. At the same time, I noticed the warm wetness on my upper lip. I swiped at it with one shaking hand, and my fingers came away bloody.

"Where's Evan?" I demanded, my voice cracking.

God, how I wanted to stand up and punish all of them, hurt them, scar them. They intended to kill my brother, the smug bastard mages.

The mages moved as one of them came forward from the back. My breath caught. It wasn't a mage. It was Evan.

But then the man's face shifted. His height changed as he went from Evan's lanky six-feet-plus to several inches shorter. Suddenly the person I was looking at was a complete stranger. I winced as if struck. It wasn't my brother. They'd used extremely strong illusion magic to fool me. I was suddenly pretty sure Jacob wasn't there, either. He'd wanted to be the one to offer up Evan, but the mages had taken my brother and cut my uncle out of their plans. He and the Steins might have been uneasy allies at some point, but I was almost sure things had changed.

"He's safe, don't worry," Sheila said, her voice throaty and cultured.

Safe? Evan was anything but safe.

Rage spilled through my veins, and I lunged at her. She twisted her hand, and the agony dialed back up. Just before I passed out, I felt a fresh gush of blood from my nose.

When I came to, it was to the sound of nearby murmurs. My head felt like my brain had been extracted, blended, and then poured back into my skull. My body didn't feel much better. It took me several seconds before I could parse the sounds into actual words.

I was upright, but not under my own power. It felt like I'd been strapped to a gurney that had been tipped up against a wall. People were talking nearby. Beneath the sound of conversation, there was the softer prattle of a TV announcer.

Instead of moving, I kept my eyes closed and my head slack. I still couldn't make out the words. I concentrated harder on picking out the voices nearest me and ignoring the TV.

". . . same blood," a young man's voice said. "Perhaps she would help ensure the seal."

"She doesn't have the right magic," another male voice said. That one I knew. It was Damien's.

"But she can act as a conduit for magic. We have proof of that," the first voice insisted.

My insides writhed against a strange, restricted feeling. Something about it felt vaguely familiar, and it sent my pulse galloping in alarm. It took a second before I remembered. Someone had placed a charm on me, one that cut me off from my magic.

"No, the soul of the reaper still resides within her," Damien argued. He spoke so rapidly I barely caught all of his words. "I've studied the magical model. Her configuration wouldn't work the same way as her brother's. Plus, her reaper could interfere. It would fight to keep her alive. Evan is the only conduit who can rid us of the interdimensional tears and safely reset the world's magic to what it was before. Anyone else would die before the job was done, dramatically raising the likelihood of unexpected effects."

They were talking about me. They were discussing possibly sacrificing me along with Evan.

"But why not hedge our bets?" the other man countered. "What does it hurt?"

"We'd run a serious risk trying to hold her until the time of the conflux," Damien said. "People will miss her. It would be difficult to keep her incapacitated for several days."

My blood went cold. Conflux? That had to be the big event, the time they planned to sacrifice Evan. And according to Damien it was still days away.

The other guy started to argue again, but Damien cut him off.

"Don't do this," Damien snapped. "It's pointless. The Order has already set the media campaigns in motion. It's already begun. They're not going to change their plans at this point. We're going with the original plan, so you might as well just drop it."

By the impatient irritated tone of Damien's voice, I guessed he was arguing with his brother. Only a sibling, or someone he had history with, would push his buttons that fast. They'd started off speaking very quietly, but as the argument had escalated, their voices had risen to the point I could hear them quite clearly. But they seemed to have realized it and had gone back to hushed whispers. I tried to keep listening and at the same time squash the panic rising up in me.

My arms were strapped down at my sides. I subtly moved my fingers, thinking maybe Damien had used charmed rings to cut me off from my magic, as he'd done before. But there were no rings. I mentally scanned the rest of my body but couldn't identify any charmed foreign object. I was trying to shift around without drawing attention, but suddenly understanding hit me like a slap in the face. I was strapped to some sort of device that not only incapacitated me physically, but also blocked my magic. The gurney or whatever they'd tied me to was one giant anti-magic charm.

I knew it was pointless, but I pushed harder, straining against the charm and searching for a weakness in it. But it was mage-made. Mages didn't make mistakes with charms like these, and even my Level III ability was no match for the block.

The effort of trying to reach for magic made my head thump, and my nose began to leak blood again. I stopped, knowing I needed to conserve my strength for something that might actually help me. Tentatively, I turned my focus within, to the center of my chest where the reaper Xaphan resided. Tuning into the subtle tug from the realm of unreaped souls, I tried reaching for the *in-between*. If I could just fade away from the land of the living, I might escape before the necromancer mage could pull me back.

I could feel limbo land out there, but I couldn't pass into it. It was like sensing a sunny day outside, but not being able to open the door and step into it. That block wasn't Damien's work. It was probably a charm from the mage who had yanked me out of the *in-between*. It was also different in that it wasn't a spell that had been tied off and left in my restraints. Whatever kept me from the *in-between* required a person there to maintain the block.

Damn. Another option cut off.

I let myself hang there limply for a long moment to gather my strength and try to figure out what to do next. Evan wasn't there, which turned out to be a small blessing because I didn't have to worry about trying to get him out with me. But who had sent the texts that had brought me to Boston? Maybe it had been Damien. It stung to think that he'd been part of the trap that landed me there, restrained and powerless. But he'd seemed to be arguing for letting me go, or at least for not killing me the way the mages were planning to kill Evan. He was only making a logical argument that killing me wouldn't benefit their efforts, but I'd take whatever I could get.

The question was, why were they still holding me?

My upper lip was starting to itch as the blood dried, interrupting my thoughts and drawing my attention back to my physical predicament. The itch intensified into a maddening tingle, and it was a small torture to not be able to wipe my nose. I couldn't help it. It was like being on the edge of a sneeze, and it was driving me nuts. I scrunched my face and inhaled sharply, trying to make the sensation stop.

But then white-hot pain stabbed through me, and my head convulsively jerked back, slamming my skull against the hard surface I was tied to. I recognized the magic searing my nerves—it belonged to Damien's mother, Sheila.

"Turn her around," Sheila said.

I cracked my eyelids open just in time to see her standing with her hand out, as if gripping an invisible tennis ball. She turned her wrist like she was twisting a dial, and the pain flared.

I groaned as a fresh flow of blood ran from my nose, and I tasted it on my lips.

"Behave yourself, and I won't need to hurt you," she said.

I nodded, and the agony dialed back. Through the pain, I took note of the subtle apprehension that edged her voice. What did she think I was going to do to misbehave while I was immobilized and cut off from my magic?

Damien and had come over to scoot me around as Sheila directed. I watched my former partner, hoping he'd look at me and I'd see some flicker of the Damien I used to know, but he kept his eyes cast down. I turned to his brother, the necromancer.

"I'm Ella," I said, my voice gravelly. "I don't think we've met."

He narrowed his eyes at me but didn't respond.

I cast a glance around the room. It was a plush office, complete with an expensive-looking desk that was polished to a reflective gleam, a high-backed chair, oak filing cabinets, and a sofa with a coffee table. There was a TV mounted on the wall I faced. Sheila and her two sons were the only ones in the room, but an interior window revealed the other mages in an adjoining office.

"So, this is the Stein family Boston headquarters?" I asked, still looking around for anything helpful. "Or maybe a branch office for the Order of Mages? Pretty mundane, needing actual office space. Can't you just astrally project and meet up that way?"

Sheila twisted her wrist, and I let out a screech as pain zipped through me.

"Quiet," she snapped. "You need to hear this."

The volume on the TV came up, and a mugshot-style photo of my brother, a recent picture, appeared on the screen.

My breath died in my throat.

I heard a door click open behind me and a few sets of shoes cross the plush carpet. The other mages, including Damien's father, had joined us. All of them were staring intently at the TV.

"There's been a shocking new development in our understanding of the Manhattan Rip and a possible solution to the interdimensional tears that have led to the disasters that claimed thousands of lives and continue to endanger the world," the clean-cut male anchor was saying. He was famous, one of the senior anchors on a major channel, but in that moment, I couldn't for the life of me remember his name. I could only stare at the photo of my brother. "A young man has come forward claiming that he has the solution. He's been working in secret for the past several years, trying to come up with some way to close the Manhattan Rip, the other permanent rips, and end the phenomenon of randomly appearing smaller rips. Now, get ready for the big twist in this almost unbelievable story. The young man who is claiming he can save the world is the nephew of Jacob Gregori, the tycoon who escaped prosecution for causing the interdimensional tears in the first place. The young man's name is Evan Grey."

The picture cut from the anchor to Evan, sitting in a chair across from the anchor in what was obviously a previously-taped interview.

My mouth fell open as Evan began to speak.

"I'm the son of Jacob Gregori's deceased brother," Evan said. His eyes were sharp, his voice clear.

"But you haven't gone by the surname Gregori, is that correct?" the anchor asked. Paul Lancing was his name.

My brother looked so . . . *normal*. Could the Steins really have gotten him cleaned up so thoroughly and so quickly?

"For obvious reasons, my mother chose a different last name, so the family connection wouldn't be obvious," Evan said. "She wanted to protect us."

No. That wasn't Evan. The cadence of the speech this look-alike used, the way he sat there with one leg crossed over the other. It wasn't my brother, it couldn't be.

"Us being your mother, your sister, and yourself?" Paul asked.

Evan nodded. "Yes, my sister Ella and I grew up with Grey as our last name."

My heart punched the inside of my chest.

The picture cut away from the interview and back to the live anchor.

"There's much more to my interview with this intriguing young man," Paul said. "But it turns out there's another story here, that of the sister Evan Grey mentioned. While Evan

Grey aims to save the world, his sister Ella Grey seems bent on helping it come undone."

My picture, the one that was on file with my old Demon Patrol precinct, appeared next to Paul's head.

"We've learned that Ella Grey aided the escape of Phillip Zarella, the scientist who was convicted of unspeakable crimes against humanity and awaiting execution. You'll remember the story that came out a few years ago, when Zarella escaped maximum security and was supposedly gunned down in his escape. Well, he wasn't killed. There was a cover-up. He went into hiding. And recently, he's been spotted. We have the entire story of the unlikely relationship between the sister of would-be hero Evan Grey and the escaped psychopath, which we'll be airing later tonight."

My photo expanded to take up almost the entire frame.

"But right now, we want to spread the word that everyone should be on the lookout for this woman, Gabriella Grey, who goes by Ella Grey. She's wanted for a several crimes, the worst of which is aiding the most notorious criminal of our time. We'll be right back with more."

The station cut to a commercial for cat food.

My head whipped over to Sheila, the sudden motion making my vision swim and nausea rise up my throat.

I stared at her in horror. "That's not my brother! This is a trick. The same illusion magic you used to lure me in here. That's not Evan! What have you done with him?"

I jerked against my restraints, nearly hyperventilating as fury and fear exploded through me.

Sheila gave me one of her cool smiles. It just about made my sanity snap in half like a piece of uncooked spaghetti.

"We'll hang onto you for a day or so, just to give the media machine a chance to build up the story to a frenzy, and then we'll turn you in," she said, her voice smooth and calm.

I twisted to look at Damien.

"How can you go along with this?" I demanded, my voice straining with anger. "It's all lies! That's not even my brother. How can you *live* with yourself, Damien? You used to be a decent person. How can you do this?"

I was shaking against my restraints, and my lower lids were filling with tears of outrage.

His demeanor seemed almost as chilly and detached as his mother's, but as he pivoted to fully face me, I thought I saw a flicker of something in his expression. It was probably too much to hope that it was a tiny signal of some inner conflict he might be feeling.

"Answer me!" I yelled, spraying spit and blood.

Everyone in the room was staring at the two of us, but the other mages seemed to be waiting for Damien's response.

Again, there was a flash of doubt in his eyes.

"Because this is the right thing to do for humanity," he said. "And we're making it so that no one else needs to feel guilty about the sacrifice. Your brother will go down in history a hero—a willing hero who knew the risk and knew it was worth it. His worthless life will mean something, Ella. He'll be a modern savior."

He nearly had me convinced. But I'd spent a lot of time with Damien. I could tell when he was reciting something rather than speaking with deep conviction. But I also knew I couldn't very well try to coax him back from the dark side while we were surrounded by his family.

My voice dropped to a harsh whisper. "And just as frosting on the cake, you're going to ruin me, too?"

Sheila stepped forward, clearly preferring to take charge of the conversation.

"We can't have you jeopardizing the plan. But with this—" she gestured gracefully to the TV with one slim arm. "You've been completely discredited. No one will believe anything you say. In fact, next to Zarella you'll soon be the most hated person in the country. Maybe the world."

She shook her head, and for a moment she almost looked genuinely sad.

"We know it's difficult for someone like you to understand," she said, her tone more condescending than pitying. "But people like us know what must be done, and more important, we're willing to do it."

Pure black hatred, anger like I'd never felt in my life, was swelling inside me like a tidal wave heading toward its inevitable crash upon the shore. But there was something else. The world looked as if it were seeping blood as crimson magic spread into the air around me. They didn't know about the blood magic. They hadn't blocked it. The inside of my nose, my upper lip, and my tongue were tingling as the magic mingled with my blood.

Some part of my mind registered that anger seemed to be a trigger for bringing forth this magic.

"You are monsters," I said, my voice a low growl. "All of you."

Sheila's eyes widened, and her icy façade began to crack as she sensed that something was happening. She couldn't see the blood magic, and neither could the others. But they knew I was drawing power. It was gathering around my hands, but they were still bound. It was also filling my mouth.

Not knowing what would happen or exactly how to wield the blood magic, I drew a deep breath, filling my lungs, and then exhaled forcefully into the room, sending the crimson magic outward, and my anger and desire to hurt the mages along with it.

The air filled with red specks, like a fine mist of blood. It hit Sheila in the face first. Her skin began to splotch, and the red areas quickly boiled into blisters. She screeched as the blisters spread over her bare arms. It was hitting the others, too, and when the mist engulfed the necromancer mage who'd been keeping me from the *in-between*, I felt a subtle release in my chest. The spell he'd been using to keep me from fading into limbo land had dissolved.

Damien's father had the presence of mind to draw air magic and try to blow back against the crimson mist, and one of the other mages began to form a magical container to trap it. In a few seconds, they'd have it contained. Now was my chance.

I ran out of breath and turned my attention inward to my reaper. Together, we reached out to the realm of souls, and I faded from the land of the living.

I knew I had maybe a few seconds before their necromancer tried to wrench me out of the *in-between.* The skeletal shape I took in limbo land was too thin to be held by the restraints. I slipped my arms out from under the straps and quickly released the ones around my chest, waist, and legs and stepped away from the gurney. I whipped around, looking for an escape. At the same time, I reached out with my senses, searching for the nearest river of underground magic—a ley line from which I could draw power. There was one in the vicinity, but it was miles away. Better than nothing.

I ran for the open doorway and burst through it, only to find myself in another room that was a dead end. Just as I wheeled around to go back the way I'd come, the center of my chest twitched as if my reaper were jerking in alarm. A second later, a ghostly figure materialized in front of me.

Damn. It was the Steins' necromancer. I had no idea how he was projecting himself into the *in-between* without the aid of a reaper soul, but the answer had to be some insanely powerful mage magic.

I reached for my chain whip, which the mages had been arrogant enough to leave on my belt. It fell to the ground like a little waterfall of metal.

"This is my realm," I growled, my voice not really my own.

My forearms met, and the sigils on them lit up with silver light as ley line magic flooded into me. It hurt like hell, but not as bad as Sheila's torture. At least with this pain, I was in charge. I didn't absolutely have to use the trick of the sigils to draw ley line magic in the *in-between*, but I knew it looked impressive and I was going for intimidation.

Silver magic sparked down the length of the whip as I flicked my wrist and sent the power-imbued razor chain flying through the air toward the necromancer's ghostly image. I wasn't sure what damage I could do, if any, to a projection, but I was willing to try every trick I had.

The necromancer raised his hands, palms out, and balls of pure white magic pulsed toward me. I quickly changed the trajectory of the whip to intercept the barrage of golf-ball sized orbs. My magic and the mage's magic clashed and sparked, seeming to burn away the gray mist.

I needed to get past this asshole. I switched the whip handle to my left hand and continued to fend off the attack. Allowing Xaphan, my reaper, to come forth, I raised my right hand. He knew what I wanted to do. The reaper's blade appeared in my hand, and I stalked toward the mage, my whip flying in a spiral to deflect his magic.

"Get out, or I'll reap you right now," I ground out, brandishing the reaping knife.

The mage's attack faltered and sputtered down to nothing. His image stumbled backward and then winked out of sight.

The knife disappeared from my hand. I let go of the ley line magic, and it receded into the ground like a serpent slithering back to its lair. With no time to gather my whip, I dragged it behind me as I sprinted through the doorway, back out another door, and flew into the hallway. Kicking up great puffs of mist, I made a wild dash down the stairs, out through the lobby, and into the eternal gray twilight of the *in-between*. I sprinted away from the Brownstone.

I couldn't have actually reaped the mage's soul, but he didn't know that. Probably wasn't a trick I'd be able to get away with again, but it had worked this time, and it had been enough. Back when Xaphan had still been trying to take over my body and mind, I would have been able to reap the souls of the living. It turned out Xaphan was kind of dirty as far as reapers went. But he and I had made a deal, an agreement to live in symbiosis with each other. Part of the deal was that he couldn't ever use my hand to reap souls of the living. I wasn't going to let him turn me into a murderer. But I'd discovered that he would let me brandish the reaping blade, and I might even say he enjoyed doing it.

There was a water feature in Boston Common, not far from where I'd exited the park. I made a turn and ran harder, aiming in what I hoped was the right direction, with my bladed whip clinking along the ground behind me.

I heard footsteps pursuing me, and my heart tried to jump up my throat. Or it would have, if I had a normal body in limbo land. Someone was gaining on me, but I couldn't go any faster. When Loki pulled even with me, I nearly crashed into a streetlight in panic before I realized it was him.

"Good boy." I gave him a little grin, and he grinned back. "Let's get the hell out of here, huh? We need water."

I wasn't sure I was going the right way and was just about to pause and pop into the realm of the living to check my map when Loki pulled ahead. He looked back at me and then veered off the street into an alley. Figuring he might have sniffed out water, I followed him.

He led me to what looked like a library or part of a university—the signage wasn't visible in this realm—and a splashing rock fountain centered on the landing after a short flight of steps. We jogged up, and I nearly reached for the water, picturing the kitchen at home in my mind.

But then I remembered my face on the news. I was wanted. Shit. I couldn't go home. And what about Deb and Roxanne? I needed a place to hide out from the authorities *and* from the mages. Rogan's old house was still vacant last time I checked. When he'd first shown me the trick with the water, he'd used a pond in the yard of one of his neighbors. I formed the image in my mind's eye and then trailed my skeletal fingers across the water in the catch basin at the bottom of the fountain.

Loki and I shifted back in Boise. Even though I knew I'd be pursued, it was a relief to be back home. I walked the half block or so to Rogan's, went around to the yard, and popped back into the living realm. I let out a relieved breath when I discovered it was dark out. I found the key hidden under a rock in the border planting area that ran along one side of the small deck, and I let myself and Loki inside.

Rogan had no next of kin, so I wasn't sure how his house was being handled. If payments stopped, I supposed the bank would eventually repossess it and sell it. But for the moment, it was still furnished with his things, and I was incredibly grateful to find the heat was still on.

Leaving the lights off, I made my way through the kitchen to the living room. I stood there in the dark, holding my phone in my hand. I couldn't power it on. The authorities would trace my location. I went to the bedroom. There on the nightstand was Rogan's phone, the burner I'd bought him. I rummaged around until I found the charger in a kitchen drawer and plugged in the device.

Dialing Deb's number from memory, I called her.

"Hello?" her voice sounded strained and tired.

"It's me," I said.

There was a shuddering inhalation. "Oh my god, Ella! What the hell is going on?"

"I'm okay," I said. "Are you alone?" I sure hoped so, seeing as how she'd just hollered my name.

"Roxanne is here, but she's asleep," she said. "What *happened*?"

"It's the mages," I said. "They're setting it up so no one will question Evan trying to close the rips, and when he dies, it will be a tragic but heroic accident. And they're obviously trying to keep me from interfering."

"This is insanity," she said shakily. It sounded like she'd started crying. "Are you safe?"

"Yeah, I think so," I said. "But I obviously can't tell you where I am. I'm assuming someone's already been there looking for me."

"Local police and some feds."

"Did they harass you?"

"They tried, but then I faked some labor pains and they backed off."

I let out a short laugh, and the sound surprised me. I wouldn't have guessed I'd even be capable of laughter at that point.

"What do you need?" she asked. "How are we going to fix this?"

"I don't know," I said truthfully. I heaved an exhausted sigh. "The mages have really screwed me."

"I'm going to talk to the coven," Deb said firmly.

I started to protest, but she cut me off.

"No, they know you're innocent. We can't take on the Order of Mages, but we're not going to just stand by while you try to do this on your own. That's not who we are."

I was going to argue but knew she'd go ahead with whatever she intended anyway.

"Okay," I said. "Just be really, really careful."

"I will. Lay low, and I'll get back to you as soon as I can."

It suddenly struck me how few people in the world would help me or defend me. I had the sudden, dizzying sensation of floating in space, not knowing which way was up and powerless to propel myself in any direction.

"Thank you, Deb," I said, squeezing my eyes closed. "But seriously, don't do anything risky. This is my problem, and you've got to think about yourself and the baby."

"You shut up right now," she said with some snap in her voice. "You're my family. I'm not going to let you do this alone. Gretchen needs her godmother."

"Gretchen?"

"Yeah, I'm naming the baby after you."

I laughed again, and it dissolved into a groan. "But I hate my middle name. Pick something else."

"No way," she said. "I've already told her. I can't take it back."

Tears sprang to my eyes, and I bit down on my lips for a second.

"Thanks, Deb," I said again.

"Love you."

"Love you too."

We hung up.

I flopped onto the sofa, and Loki jumped up next to me. I needed to get him a dish of water, but I didn't have the strength to get up. Running my hand over the fabric, I peered around the dark room. The very spot where I was sitting was where Evan had laid bundled in a blanket after Rogan and I had saved him from the vampire feeder den. The recliner nearby was where Rogan had kept watch over my brother. This was the last place I'd seen Rogan alive.

I sighed and pushed away the sadness that threatened to well up. I didn't have time for grief. I stood, pulled all the curtains, and then switched on the TV and turned to the local channel most likely to be playing news at this hour. I tried to steel myself for what I'd see and hear, but it was still a shock to find my face and name splashed all over the updates.

When they played a clip from the national news interview with "Evan," I moved closer to the screen and sat down on the carpet right in front of it, crossing my legs and peering up at the TV like a child.

I shook my head slowly, more certain there was no way that person was Evan, even though he looked identical to my brother. That type of illusion magic was on par with the teleportation that Damien had done. Was it my former partner who posed as my brother in the interview? They were about the same build. It would be less work, magically speaking, for someone who was similar in stature to illusion himself into a copy of Evan.

When the news moved on to a different story about a local charity, I let my face fall into my hands.

The mages believed it was just to kill my brother in the name of saving lives. Even my own uncle agreed, though he was selfishly motivated to some degree. Jacob wanted to atone for the sins of his company, for opening the rips in the first place. He *had* been responsible. He'd all but admitted it to me. And he was fine with sacrificing Evan.

The powerful people in this world just sucked. Maybe Zarella was right. We should let chaos reign and allow the world to unravel itself. As a species, we probably deserved it.

But Evan didn't deserve to be a sacrificial lamb. That was really the only thing I gave a shit about anymore. Well, that and giving Deb's baby a chance to grow up in a decent world. And Deb the opportunity for happiness. And Roxanne . . .

Well, shit. I supposed I did care about a few things after all.

"Someday, we're going to get the hell out of there," I said to Loki. "We'll find a nice quiet place in the mountains and live like old coots, Switchboard style."

My dog's tail thumped against the sofa cushion.

For no reason that I could discern, my thoughts suddenly skipped to Caleb Montgomery, the tall, good-looking, green-eyed Supernatural Crimes guy I'd sort of promised to meet up with this weekend. Was it already the weekend? I'd lost track of the days. Not that it mattered. By then he was probably counting his lucky stars that he hadn't actually gone out with me.

Maybe he'd come to mind because that night he'd kissed me outside the bar was one of the few semi-normal moments I'd had in ages. It could very well be the last normal thing that ever happened to me.

I lay down and curled up on my side. I was chilly but too tired to get up for a blanket. With the flickering monitor and the soft drone of late-night TV lulling my senses, I dropped into sleep.

I awoke suddenly, and it was still dark out when I sat up, stiff from having slept on the floor. Sleep must have allowed my subconscious to work on my predicament because a plan had formed with such clarity it almost seemed as if it were divine intervention.

I fumbled into the kitchen to put on a pot of coffee, and while I waited for it to percolate, I began typing a message into Rogan's phone. My plan depended on Phillip Zarella's help. He'd cut me off because I'd gone against him when I'd flitted off to San Francisco. But ultimately, my impulsive action hadn't really messed things up too much. The mages intended to sacrifice Evan at the "conflux" Damien had mentioned, and I was almost positive it was a specific place and time when the conditions were right to do so. He'd said it was days away. They were obviously trying to lay a foundation through the media so that when Evan died closing the rips no one would suspect that he hadn't gone willingly. That kind of story took time to infiltrate the mind of the public. I had a little bit of breathing room, but not much. And I still didn't know exactly when and where the big event would take place.

It might take some begging to get back in Zarella's good graces, but I'd do whatever it took. And this time, I was going to be in charge.

I was a fugitive after the Steins made sure my face got splashed all over the news, and there wasn't much I could do about that. I had to hide out, but it didn't mean I was stuck. I could still have eyes out in the world. I could travel by way of the *in-between* and post minor demons wherever I wanted to keep watch for me, if necessary. But I wanted zombies. As many as possible. I wanted an undead army at my back when the time came to thwart the mages. That was where I needed Zarella and any other necromancers who were willing to help.

I also needed magical knowledge, the type of academic understanding that Damien had spent his life mastering. He'd talked about a "conflux" when he was arguing with his brother, and it was exactly the sort of nerd-magic term Damien liked to use. In fact, I'd heard him talk about such things before. I would bet whatever meager balance remained in my bank account that the conflux was a combination of conditions that would magically amp up what the mages wished to accomplish. It probably involved the phase of the moon, proximity to a ley line and possibly a sacred place, maybe a significant pagan holiday, and other magical factors. I didn't have time to reach his level of expertise, though. I'd have to rely on others who knew about that sort of thing, as well as whatever my spies could glean, to figure out exactly when and where the mages would try to kill my brother.

I couldn't turn on my own phone to get the last phone number Zarella had used to contact me. Instead, I logged into an email account that I knew he would recognize. I typed a quick message that said I'd learned my lesson and wouldn't jump the gun again. I fibbed a little, saying I knew when and where the mages planned to sacrifice Evan. I didn't have that info yet, but I'd get it in time. I had no other choice. And it was my one bargaining chip with Zarella.

I suspected the madman and his cronies intended to swoop in at the last minute and snatch Evan. That was why they'd been watching and waiting, instead of just taking my brother and hiding him. They probably planned to do something that would cause even more chaos. Maybe they had their own magic they intended to toss into the mix to try to trigger some big bomb of darkness to explode into the world. The more I considered it, the more likely it seemed.

So. I had the mages to deal with, as well as Zarella and his people. There was one other faction that had designs on Evan—my uncle Jacob. It seemed as if the mages had undercut what he'd intended, which last I knew was to use my brother to close the rips and take credit for himself and

Gregori Industries. Jacob wasn't used to feeling powerless. But Zarella had Jacob backed into a corner. And my uncle was no match for the mages. Maybe I could leverage my uncle to aid my cause, but I wasn't even sure I needed him.

For one brief moment, I felt like an evil genius standing there in the dark and scheming over my mug of coffee. But evil genius manipulations were about as out of character as I could get, and I couldn't take anything for granted.

With the message off to Zarella and nothing to do there but await a response, I turned my attention to the magical problem I had to solve: discovering when and where the mages would hold the conflux.

The collective knowledge of my coven should be able to help. Deb had said to wait for her to call back, but I was antsy. I dialed her number, but she didn't pick up. I disconnected when her voice mail recording began to play.

I still had the phone in my hand when it rang.

"Hello?"

"It's me," came Deb's voice. "I bought one of those throwaway phones. I figured it would be safer."

"Good idea," I said. "Hey, I need you and the other witches. I can't believe I'm requesting this, but could you possibly do an emergency meeting of the coven? If you can gather everyone, I'll use the *in-between* to get there."

"Already got you covered," she said. "We're meeting in an hour, but not at Lynnette's. That's too likely a place for the authorities to come looking for you, especially if they see the rest of us gathering."

"Awesome," I said, already feeling uplifted. "Where are we going?"

"Becky's parents have a loft downtown," she said. "They're out of the country right now, so the place is free. It's really secure. There's a desk with a security guard and everything. So even if someone spots us going in and makes the connection to you, the police won't be able to get past the lobby without a warrant."

"Nice," I said appreciatively. "You'll just have to give me a good visual so I can picture it."

"I'll send you the address, and Becky said she's got some pics from Christmas that show the living room. Will that be enough?"

"Should be," I said. "Only one way to find out."

"Okay, she's going over there soon, and the rest of us will follow in a bit. I'll ask her to set up a glass of water in a corner and send you a pic. You can go whenever you want."

My attention perked up. A chance to talk to Becky alone before the others showed up? Yes, please. Taking down Lynnette was secondary to the bigger problem of saving my brother, but I hadn't forgotten.

Unexpectedly, I felt a small grin creep over my face. "Thank you, Deb. I can't tell you how much this means."

"What? Are you saying you're grateful for the coven?" she asked with exaggerated shock.

"I am," I admitted. "But mostly for you. I don't know what I'd do without you."

"Ditto," she said, and I could hear the smile in her voice.

We hung up, and a moment later Rogan's phone pinged with a couple of incoming text messages—the address and pictures Deb had promised.

I studied the pictures as well as the location of Becky's parents' building for a couple of minutes. Then I ran water in my empty coffee mug and set it on the counter.

It was a relief to leave the living behind and fade to the *in-between*, where I could roam without worrying I'd be recognized. Hell, I didn't even have to worry about conversing with anyone, let alone running into trouble with the authorities. I stood there in Rogan's kitchen for a moment, just savoring the peace of limbo land. When Loki appeared next to me, I knew I shouldn't linger any more. I needed to take advantage of a few minutes alone with Becky.

Deb sent me a picture of a vase full of water in the corner of Becky's parents' living room.

Recalling the images I'd just memorized, I used the bit of water in the mug to transport us. Belatedly, I realized I should have had Deb warn Becky that I would be appearing out of nowhere momentarily. I hesitated as I stood next to the vase in the room filled with gray mist but then decided to trust that my best friend had given Becky the proper heads up.

I allowed the tug of the living realm to pull me back.

I squinted and shaded my eyes against the sudden brightness of the overhead lights.

Becky was at the kitchen island on the far side of the open space. We both jumped when we saw each other. I was startled because I hadn't been expecting that entire end of the room, as it hadn't been visible in the photos. She was startled, well, presumably because a woman and a hellhound doodle had just materialized in front of her.

She pressed a hand to her chest. "I knew to expect it, and you still scared me," she said with a self-conscious laugh.

"Sorry," I said. I walked around the big sectional to join her in the kitchen area. "I hope you don't mind I'm early."

She shook her head. "Not at all. I'm glad, actually."

Becky had always been one of the more aloof members of the coven, as much as any of us could get away with being so, which was probably why I'd never sensed she might be an ally against Lynnette. She'd never seemed to display the rapt devotion of some of the women, nor did she ever appear to have any issues with our coven leader.

She appeared put-together, with a stylishly tousled long blond bob, tailored clothes, and subtle but tasteful makeup. Lynnette had hand-picked the members of the coven, most of them for the unique magical talents they offered, but I wasn't aware of anything Becky could do that was much out of the ordinary.

I leaned a hip against the counter and stuffed my fists in my jacket pockets. Loki was busily sniffing everything in the expansive space.

"I feel a little strange that you and I have never talked much in the four or five months I've been with the coven," I said.

Becky wiped her hands on a floral kitchen towel and then folded it and placed it neatly on the granite counter. Then she placed both hands on the countertop and leaned on it, giving me a shrewd look.

"It's always the quiet ones who are secretly subversive," she said, her lips widening into a conspiratorial smile. Her gray-green eyes sparked, and I couldn't help grinning back.

It suddenly struck me that perhaps her tasteful but bland appearance lulled people into thinking exactly what I'd always assumed—she was nice and attractive, but nothing about her particularly raised your interest. I knew she had some family money and a college degree, but beyond those facts and her accounting background, I couldn't say much else about her.

"So, how did your, uh, current train of thought about Lynnette begin?" I asked carefully.

"There are a few of us in the coven who've recently suspected she wasn't exactly being honest about certain aspects of the finances," she said. "It was the supposed angel benefactor that really got us going. I mean, it was pretty ridiculous."

I raised my hands skyward in a hallelujah gesture. "*Thank* you! Finally, someone else who sees that crap for what it is. Who else have you been talking to?"

She bit her bottom lip for a second. "I can't say. Not yet."

"I get it." A brief frown passed over my face. "I wish I'd known earlier, though. I thought I was the only one in the coven who wasn't buying into her antics. It made me slightly crazy at times."

"Don't get me wrong," Becky said. "You and I are in the minority. Lynnette has several *very* solid supporters in the coven. We assumed Deb was one of them."

She paused as if expecting me to respond, even though it wasn't exactly phrased as a question.

I pushed my fingers into my hair. "Yeah, I've tried to talk to her about it, but . . . it didn't go well."

Those discussions had nearly driven a huge, ugly wedge between me and Deb, so I'd had to back off.

Becky nodded. "We couldn't approach you, even though we figured you'd probably align with us, because we weren't certain about Deb, and everyone knows how close the two of you are. We have to be very careful."

I sighed. "Understandable. So, how can I help? What's your plan with the coven elections?"

She spread her hands. "Basically, we just need you to back out of your nomination. It's imperative I get that position, so I can dig into Lynnette's records. I've even got a friend who specializes in forensic accounting, if needed."

"I'm glad to withdraw, but that's easy. I really want to *help*."

She scrunched her mouth to one side, and I thought she'd decline my offer, but then she grinned again. "We might need you to use your reaper trick . . . to spy on her."

"Now we're talking," I said. "Just let me know when and where."

Her expression turned serious. "Ella, about the reports on the news. I know it's not true. The rest of the women do, too. Deb explained about your brother and how your old partner kidnapped him for the mages. She said they somehow faked his interview, and—"

I held up a hand and cut her off with a groan. "God, please stop. It sounds absolutely insane when you say it all out loud. *I* wouldn't believe Deb if I were you, to be honest. It makes me feel guilty that you're all . . . just so . . ." I shrugged helplessly, not knowing exactly what I was trying to say.

She waited patiently for a second or two to see if I was going to pull my shit together and finish the sentence. When I didn't, she folded her hands on the counter and tilted her head.

"Well, we did a little research of our own, and we as a coven are satisfied that Deb is telling the truth."

"Even Lynnette?" I didn't bother trying to hide my incredulity.

She rolled her eyes. "Who knows. But she's acting the part, anyway. I'm fairly certain the rest of the women are on your side. I am."

I passed a hand over my eyes, which were annoyingly tingly with the threat of misting up. "I seriously don't even know what to say. Except thank you."

A pleasant trill of chimes sounded, and Loki took off in what I assumed was the direction of the front door. I pulled myself together as Becky went to answer it.

I watched carefully as Becky greeted each of the four witches who came in, trying to discern whether any of them were her allies. But soon I was pulled into conversations and couldn't keep a close eye on how our hostess was interacting with everyone. Most of them arrived with laptops, books, and even the odd file folder or rolled-up papers. Deb had told them the nature of my need—figuring out when and where to intercept the mages to save my brother from certain death.

The women all seemed genuinely relieved to see me and sympathetic to my situation. Or they did a good job of acting that way. I didn't believe for a second that Lynnette wanted to deal with my problems. She was interested in power and money, and my current notoriety probably wouldn't bring either. If anything, she was probably trying to figure out a way to get rid of me. Or maybe even turn me in, if there was something in it for her. Regardless, she gave me a hug and clucked over me along with everyone else.

Once all the members had arrived and most were caught up in various conversations, I pulled Deb away from the group.

"Are you okay?" I asked.

"I should be asking you that, not the other way around," she said.

"I'm not the one who's pregnant," I said.

She shook her head and gave an exasperated look. "Gretchen and I are fine. You're the target of a national manhunt."

I pulled a horrified face. "Is that what they're calling it?"

She grimaced. "Yeah, and guess who was the first to throw the term out there? The Order of Mages. It's so obvious they're pulling the strings behind all the media stuff."

I blew out a slow breath, trying to calm the churning in my stomach. "It's obvious to you only because you know the truth."

My gaze slid back to the group. Lynnette was gathering everyone in the seating area. She probably had a speech prepared. Well, I had some things to say, too.

I stood at the edge of the group, and before Lynnette could open her mouth, I started talking.

"I'd like to say a few things, if you don't mind." I paused to glance at Lynnette but didn't wait for her permission. "First of all, I know you've taken a risk just to be here in the same room with me. You probably have family members and friends who know I'm part of your coven and are wondering what the hell is going on. They're probably worried about you and how my problems will blowback on you. I don't blame anyone for those reactions. But your loyalty, your being here right now, means the world to me."

I paused for a breath. I don't think I'd ever said so many words at once in a coven meeting.

"You did save all our asses when the baelmen attacked," Elena piped up. She pulled her thick, chestnut hair over her shoulder and gave me her signature sassy look. "So, you know, we owe you our firstborns and all that."

A few of the women smiled or laughed softly.

I shook my head. "You really don't, but thank you for that. Before I get into the reason we're here, I want to formally withdraw my candidacy for Keeper of Means. Obviously, I've got a little too much on my plate to take on such an important position in the coven right now."

I glanced at Lynnette, and she acknowledged my withdrawal by inclining her head. I thought she might try to take the floor, but she just folded her arms, seemingly content to let me continue.

"Okay," I said. "This is where I could really use your help. The mages are going to sacrifice my brother, but they're going to wait until the right moment and choose the right location that will be optimal for what they intend. I need you to help me figure out when and where that's going to be. All I know is that we're only days away from the event, so we're talking near future. That's our starting point."

Lynnette stepped forward. "All right, ladies, let's divide into two groups. One will work on figuring out the intended time of the sacrifice, and the other will work on figuring out the place. Time group works here around the coffee table, and the location group can work at the kitchen island."

There was a flurry of movement as the women shuffled themselves around to divide into two working groups and then began powering up their laptops, opening worn leather-bound tomes and sifting through the notebooks and stacks of papers.

I went over to the location group and stood next to Jen. She bumped me with her hip.

"Hey, girl," she said. "We're going to nail this, you know that, right?"

"You'd better," I said, cracking a grim smile. "You guys are my best shot."

The witches quickly got down to work. I'd assumed that figuring out the location would be the more difficult of the two tasks because the possibilities were practically infinite whereas the timing was somewhat bound already, and I expected factors such as celestial events would help narrow it down considerably. As I listened to the women toss out possible locations, I realized I was probably right.

They formed a list of about thirty locations around the world with known heightened magical capacity or features that could be used to power up spells.

"Okay, but wait," Jen said. "Do the mages have to use one of the major rips for this? Because that would mean Manhattan, Boise, or the couple of other places with large, permanent interdimensional tears."

She looked at me, and I shook my head. "I don't know. We have to assume they have the power to open their own very large rip if they want to."

My eyes involuntarily flicked to Lynnette. For a while, she'd been creating small interdimensional tears herself in order to collect the rip magic that formed around them. It was very dangerous, not to mention illegal. But if a Level II like Lynnette could do it, there was no doubt the mages could also do it, and on a much bigger scale if they wanted to.

"But what would be the advantage of doing that?" Elena asked. "Why open a new one if there are plenty of big ones already existing?"

"Maybe none of the existing ones are in the right locations," suggested one of the women. "Or maybe they need it to be fresh or have some other custom-made characteristic we don't know about."

The group was silent for a long moment.

"If that's the case, then we're back to square one," Jen said. "It could be just about anywhere."

"Let's go down our list and try to rate the likelihood of each location," Elena said.

For the next forty-five minutes, we did just that. But the exercise didn't seem to get us any closer to an answer. The mood of the group had turned decidedly gloomy.

"Anybody have any other ideas?" Jen asked. After a few seconds, she suggested we take a short break.

A few of the others and I wandered over to edge of the timing group. As expected, they seemed to be making a lot more progress. They'd identified two dates within the next two weeks that were most advantageous for carrying out magical activities, as well as a handful of dates that were weaker candidates but still carried enough significance to be considered.

Elena stood next to me. Without looking at me, she began speaking softly.

"My grandmother was born in Mexico, in a town with strong magic and even stronger witches," she said. "She always told me the gut knows. Listen to the gut first for the answer. Then check the heart and then the head." Her hand moved up from her lower belly to her chest to her temple as she spoke. "What does your gut say about the location they'll pick?"

I chewed my lip for a moment, letting my awareness drift away from my churning mind and settle in my stomach.

"I think it'll be here." The words just popped out. Up to that second, I hadn't felt any certainty about it. But once I said it out loud, it made sense. "I think it will be done at the Boise Rip."

"How come?" Jen asked. She was standing on my other side and had been listening to Elena.

I thought for a minute. "It's one of the largest rips besides the Manhattan one, but unlike the original rip, the Boise Rip is in a more isolated area and not as heavily guarded, so it'll be much simpler for them to access it," I said. I kept my voice low, so I wouldn't disrupt the other group's flow. "But that's not the most important part. In terms of magically active places, there's really nothing special about Manhattan. That rip formed there because that's where Gregori Industries was located, and that's where their experiments went wrong. But this area is a magical hotbed. That's presumably why we ended up with our own permanent rip."

I paused for a couple of seconds, and a small sigh escaped my lips. "And, I know for a fact the local magical activity is what drew Damien here," I finished.

Elena and Jen's eyes were glued on me as they took in what I was saying. When I went silent, they looked at each other. Jen stepped away and began rounding up our group again. Once we were gathered around the kitchen island, she asked me to repeat what I'd said.

There were slow nods and some murmurs of agreement. We talked it over for a few minutes.

"What are we going to do about it?" Jen asked.

I tilted my head. "It?"

She spread her hands in a gesture that took in our group and the women gathered around the coffee table. "So we figure out when and where the mages plan to toss your brother into the abyss. What are we going to do about it?"

I puffed my cheeks out and then blew a slow breath while I shook my head. "I don't expect you guys to put yourselves in danger. Evan is my responsibility."

She gave me a challenging look and lifted her chin. "Okay, what's your plan, then?"

I scratched my forehead. "Uh, I hadn't figured that out yet."

"But you thought you'd just swoop in there all alone and grab him?" She lifted an eyebrow at me, clearly skeptical.

I lifted my hands and then let my arms drop to my sides, my shoulders slumping a little. The oracle had warned me that I couldn't save Evan solo. It was my instinct to go it alone, but I would only get one shot. If following the dragon's advice upped my odds against the mages, I had to do it.

"Okay. No, you're actually right," I said. "I can't do it alone. But I also don't want to get all of you killed. I don't expect the entire coven to pitch in on this one."

Jen opened her mouth to argue, but Lynnette cut her off, calling to us from the other group.

"Hey ladies, we think we've got something," Lynnette said. She waved us over.

We all crowded around. I recognized Deb's neat writing on the pages of notes that were spread over the coffee table.

Becky lifted up one of the sheets. At the top, there was a date in block letters—January 31—and underneath a written bullet list. That date was less than a week away.

"We think this is it," Lynnette said, pointing to Becky's piece of paper. "It's the night of the full moon, and this year it's the Quickening Moon. It usually falls in February, but this year it's in January. The Quickening Moon is powerful for magic of endings and new beginnings. That date is also smack in the middle of a trine between Neptune, the planet of illusion, and Mars, the planet of power. It's a rare configuration. Even more overt, there's also a sextile between Jupiter and Mercury."

I squinted, trying to recall what little I knew about astrology, but I was coming up short. By the pointed looks being exchanged among the women, though, the astrological events Lynnette described were extremely significant.

She held up a finger. "One more thing. The icing on the cake. There's a lunar eclipse." A couple of the witches gasped. "It's a partial one, but partial eclipses are nearly as powerful as full eclipses."

Certainty pinged through me like a cold little marble of ice. This had to be the date. Damien would have been able to run calculations on all of this information. Probabilities. Models. The thought that he was using his knowledge against me brought a pang of sadness to my heart. I pushed it away. He was the expert, but his way wasn't the only way.

"Did you identify anything related to the time that might favor certain areas? Like specific altitudes or things like that?" I asked. It was the sort of thing Damien would try to tease out, too.

Lynnette's jet-black brows shot up, and she gave a short laugh. "Yes, in fact. The eclipse is most powerful along these longitudes." She tapped one of the lines toward the bottom of the sheet. Deb had written a row of numbers there.

"Guess where one of those longitudes passes through," Becky said.

A grim smile had already started to make its way over my lips. "Right here in Idaho."

Jen and I quickly presented our group's conclusion.

"Our take was obviously less methodical than yours, and we don't have the data to back it up the way you do," I said. I glanced at Elena. "Our task didn't work that way. We had to use some gut instinct. But I think you just confirmed our best guess."

Jen let out a raucous, guttural, "Yeah!"

The other witches joined in, clapping and whooping, and I couldn't hold back a broad grin. When Deb got up and came toward me, I held out my hands in defense.

"No!" I said, laughing as tears of relief sprang to my eyes. "If you hug me right now, I'll lose it."

She stuck out her tongue but stayed where she was.

"Thank you," I said, my gaze sweeping the faces around me. "You all have been amazing."

"You've really gone above and beyond," Lynnette said, stepping up next to me and drawing the group's attention. "If any of you need to go, now's your chance. The rest of us will stay behind to discuss what's next."

"Wait," I said, moving half a step in front of Lynnette. "Before anyone takes off, I have a question. I don't expect anyone to know the answer, but I'd like to hear your theories." There I went, using Damien-speak again. "How do you think the mages will compel my brother, the real Evan, into the rip? I mean, it'll have to look convincing, so they can't drug him. Do mages have mind control magic? Could they command him like a necromancer drives a zombie?"

"Some sort of verbal magic would be my guess," Lynnette said after a couple of seconds passed and no one said anything. "Maybe a binding promise combined with a very strong suggestive spell."

My heart clenched as I imagined my brother's mind being manipulated by people more powerful by orders of magnitude. The cruelty of it sent a surge of anger through me. I tamped it down. The coven didn't deserve my wrath. I'd save it for the Steins.

"So it probably won't be only a matter of trying to physically rescue him," I said quietly, doing my best to keep my voice even. "I'll have to break the magic hold the mages will have on his mind."

The mood in the room sobered quickly.

"Sorry to be such a buzzkill," I said with a humorless laugh.

The women cast sympathetic looks at me.

"Why don't we break for fifteen, and anyone who needs to go can do so," Lynnette suggested.

While everyone was milling around, Becky sidled over to me. She pasted on a pleasant smile and flicked a glance over at Lynnette before speaking.

"We're still having our regular coven meeting in two days," she said. "We're going to be voting. After that, I plan to move very quickly with the records."

"I might need her, though," I whispered, trying not to move my mouth much in case Lynnette happened to look our way and decided to attempt lipreading. "She's got skills with rips and rip magic."

"I'll keep that in mind," Becky said and then moved away toward the kitchen island.

Keep in it mind? This was my brother's life. Coven politics, even gross wrongdoing on the part of our leader, were *not* more important than Evan.

I frowned at Becky's retreating back but then smoothed my expression before anyone took notice. Seizing a moment to myself, I pulled out Rogan's phone and checked the email account I'd used to write to Zarella. Maybe he'd have some ideas about how to break Evan away from the mages' influence.

My pulse thumped when I saw he'd replied. I scanned the short message. He said he'd send someone to speak with me later that night at Rogan's house. A shiver crawled up my spine when it hit me that Zarella knew where I'd stayed the previous night. He had no reason to turn me in, but still. It meant he had eyes on me. Minor demons, maybe a zombie. I shivered again.

I didn't bother replying. I'd be there, and he knew it.

Lynnette called us back to order in her usual authoritative fashion, even though this wasn't an official coven meeting.

"I'm working on a plan for how we might help Ella grab her brother when the time comes," she said.

My brows lowered in a slight frown. I hadn't expected her to be so gung-ho about jumping in. Not that I didn't appreciate her initiative, in a way, but what was her angle? Lynnette always had one. In the past, she'd been willing to put herself in danger to acquire illegal magic or to try to gain fame for herself and the coven.

"It'll be risky, of course," she said. "And I don't have it all detailed out yet, but I'll be asking for a few of you to volunteer to help. Think about it. There's no shame in saying no. We all know Ella won't hold our choices against us."

She turned a magnanimous smile on me, and I couldn't do anything but force a smile in return. But inside, my stomach gave a twist. I was caught. I knew I needed help to save Evan, but it seemed as if anyone who might aid me had their own motives for getting involved. Zarella and Lynnette were two of the most dangerous people I knew, and yet there I was, depending on them in the most important thing I'd ever done. The oracle had told me that I'd need to turn an adversary into an ally. How about a couple of them? Would I get double points? The thing was, neither Lynnette nor Zarella would ever be true allies. They'd only help me for their own gain, as part of their own schemes. I couldn't fool myself. They weren't really on my side. The two of them weren't going to fulfill the second requirement the dragon had given me.

I touched my temple as a headache began to form across my forehead. What had the oracle said? Loki and I alone weren't enough. I needed to turn an adversary into an ally. And the rips needed to be closed, and someone would have to die to accomplish that feat.

Lynnette had continued speaking, but when I realized she was doing it mostly to reassert her authority, I partially tuned her out.

"We'll reconvene for our regular meeting here in two days, since this seems to be a secure place to meet," she said. She turned her kohl-lined eyes on me. "Will you be able to stay safe and out of sight until then?"

I nodded, but I was suddenly too tired to even form a response or express any more gratitude. What I really wished for was Rogan. He'd have jumped in to help me without a second thought, and with his reaper soul and mage magic, I wouldn't have had to worry about him getting hurt. A dizzying pang of loss spiraled through me, sudden and severe enough to make my breath hitch in my throat.

Fortunately, the witches were standing, moving around, and gathering their things as they prepared to depart, and no one seemed to notice I'd just emotionally gut-punched myself.

Well, someone noticed. As everyone else chatted or drifted toward the door, Deb came my way.

"Hey," she said quietly. "Your aura is basically one big sad-face emoji."

A ghost of a smile passed over my lips. "I just don't know if I can really depend on anyone," I whispered, not wanting the others to hear. "Except you, of course."

"What do you mean?" she asked. "The coven genuinely wants to help."

My eyes flicked to Lynnette and then back to Deb's sincere blue gaze. Right. Deb still believed Lynnette was one of the good guys.

"Yeah, I know," I said. I cleared my throat. "It's just, I don't want any of them to get hurt. None of them have ever faced mages before. It's suicidal."

"Nah," she said. "Lynnette will come up with something. She's skilled and incredibly resourceful. She wouldn't put together a suicide mission."

Wouldn't she, though? Sure, Lynnette would look out for herself, but she'd inadvertently gotten a former coven member killed. I couldn't argue, though. Not at that moment. I'd tried too many times before to get Deb to see the truth about Lynnette. It wasn't the time to try to take that up again.

I forced another smile.

"Oh, before I forget, I brought you some things," Deb said. "Some spare clothes and food for Loki."

She went and got two plastic shopping bags that sat on the floor next to her purse, bending a little awkwardly around her pregnant belly to pick it up. She came back and held out the handles so I could take them.

"There are a few other things for you in there, too," she said. "Just some essentials."

I glimpsed a foil packet that probably contained food, as well as a can of honey roasted peanuts, a bottle of my favorite lager from the fridge, a bag of Cheetos, two apples, and what looked like a peanut butter and jelly sandwich in a zip baggie. There were also a dollar store travel toothbrush and toothpaste, and some other mini toiletry items. I nearly teared up at the sight of these few small comforts.

I couldn't take that much stuff with me through the *in-between*, but I didn't want to remind Deb of that, not after she'd been so thoughtful. I'd grab a bite and change clothes before I left Becky's and see if she'd let me keep the things there until the coven meeting.

The witches trickled out the door, eventually leaving just me and Becky.

I held up the bags. "Mind if I change clothes and then leave the rest of this stuff here?"

She waved toward one of the doorways. "Not at all. That bedroom has an on-suite bathroom. You're welcome to use the shower. I'm going to clean up and then head home but take your time. You can even stay here, if you'd like."

I softened at her generous offer. I shouldn't have been so quick to get irritated earlier.

"Thank you, that means a lot," I said. "But I've got a place to stay, and I don't want to run the risk of causing problems for your family. It's enough that you're allowing us to meet here."

She waved a hand and scoffed, brushing off my worries. "My dad would have a field day if the authorities tried to bust in here. In fact, he'd probably enjoy it if they did."

"He's a lawyer, I take it?"

She arched a brow. "How'd you know?"

I snorted a laugh. "Just a lucky guess."

I went and used the shower, relishing the heat of the water and just how normal yet somehow also luxurious it felt to bathe, twist my wet hair up into a bun, and put on clean clothes. When I got out, Becky was gone. I poured Loki's food into a bowl and set it on the floor and ate the sandwich Deb had made for me. It was incredibly tempting to pop open the beer, but I still had a meeting that night and didn't want anything to dull my senses.

While I was rinsing out Loki's bowl, I got a text from Deb: *I forgot to mention it before I left (dang pregnancy brain!), but you need healing. I can tell you're depleted again. I will arrange a time for you to pop into Gina's.*

I texted back: *I don't want to get her mixed up in my mess.*

Deb's reply came right away: *She can say no if she wants to. I don't think she will, though.*

Okay. Thank you for looking out for me, I responded.

Always.

I tucked my phone away and called Loki over as I ran some water in his empty bowl. We shifted from the realm of

the living to limbo land, and I used the water to take us back
to Rogan's for my appointment with the madman.

I arrived back in Rogan's dark kitchen, with Loki appearing next to me a second or two later. I zipped up my jacket as the chill of the cooler space began to seep through my clothes, suddenly realizing just how comfortable and luxurious the warm, safe downtown penthouse had felt. A quick check of the time on Rogan's phone showed I had less than ten minutes until the meeting.

I went to the living room window that faced the back yard and peered out into the night. I didn't see anyone, but that didn't mean there weren't spies lurking nearby. Switching to necro-vision, I reached out to a minor demon I had stationed at the edge of the property, nestled in the boughs of a pine tree. Any other necromancer would sense my little spy, but there wasn't much I could do about that. I probed into the creature's brain to check out what it could see. The demon seemed agitated, and I sensed a handful of other minor demons perched in a neighbor's yard. The way they were lined up, I suspected the creatures were sitting in a row on the fence. Something about the way they were so evenly spaced out made me suspect they'd been placed there by Zarella, or perhaps one of his associates.

Something larger pinged the edge of my senses, and I automatically angled right to peer at that side of the back yard, even though I knew whatever was coming was still out of sight. As it drew closer, I recognized the feel of it—a zombie. So Zarella was sending one of his proxies, rather than coming to meet me himself. I wasn't really surprised.

Loki began pacing near the back door, a low growl rumbling in his throat.

"It's okay, boy," I whispered. "I'm expecting it."

The zombie appeared around the corner of the house, presumably having come into the yard using the side gate. A shiver spilled down my spine as I reached for the doorknob. Zombies. Blech.

The creature had stopped at the far end of the cement slab patio, standing unnaturally still as only a zombie could. The distinct smell of sage-scented magic hit me when I got within ten feet of the creature. It took very strong magic to cover the smell, which was violently stomach-turning when completely unmasked. The zombie didn't look decayed, though. The outer appearance of the zombie's body was preserved and dressed in jeans, a winter coat over a ski sweater, and sneakers. In the dark the zombie would pass for a living man. From a distance, anyway. Too close, and the smell of the magic would give him away. I had a sudden and absurd flash of curiosity about who picked out the zombie's outfit and whether the clothes were new or second-hand. How did one decide how to dress a zombie?

I gave myself a mental slap. *Focus.*

I stopped a good six feet away from the creature. I didn't need strong whiffs of the zombie-smell the sage was barely covering up. Not to mention that if Zarella happened to lose control of the zombie, it could infect or even kill me if I were caught off guard. There was a good reason why it was illegal to keep zombies animated. Set free or in the hands of an inexperienced necromancer, a zombie could quickly decimate an entire neighborhood.

The creature opened its mouth, and Zarella's words came out.

"It hurts, doesn't it?" he asked.

I tilted my head. "What?"

"Getting blamed for setting me free when it was actually Damien Stein who aided my escape and ensured that Jacob Gregori no longer had the leverage to keep me prisoner on his company's grounds," he said.

I'd known Damien had made a trade with Zarella. Mage power for my former partner, apparently in return for helping the madman gain his freedom. But I'd never known how they'd managed to force Jacob to let Zarella go.

"What was in that box that Damien retrieved for you?" I asked.

"Concrete proof of Jacob's personal role in causing the Manhattan Rip," the zombie said. "Enough to make a conviction stick this time."

"He was already tried and found not guilty," I said.

"My information would provide a slightly different path to conviction," he said, his tone growing impatient and clipped. "It shows the viruses originated from Gregori Industries. But that's irrelevant to our discussion this evening."

Zarella seemed to be in a bad mood.

"Where and when is the sacrifice to take place?" he asked.

Ah, there it was. He was annoyed that I knew something he didn't. I managed to suppress a grim smile.

"I can't tell you," I said. "Not unless I know for sure that you aren't going to make things worse. Open more rips. Cause more disease and destruction."

"What do you care? You'll have your brother, and the world will go on. We've learned to live with these interdimensional tears and the consequences of them. Look around you, Ella. Vampires get implants and live as normal people. Zombies are all destroyed or well-controlled. New infections of either virus are extremely rare. And you know from your former job that the pesky minor demons that come through occasionally can be controlled. Arch-demons are infrequent, and possessions even more so. Stop worrying about making the world into some false vision of perfection from the past.

This is the world *now*. Just embrace it and move on with your brother and your life."

"Fine, I don't need to tell you," I said mildly and crossed my arms.

The zombie took a couple of steps forward, its fists clenched at its sides.

"Yes, you do," it said. "You need me and the others, and you know it."

I reached for my whip and used earth and air magic to unfurl it from its pouch. The links clinked to the cement. I didn't know whether the zombie's threatening stance was just show from Zarella, a carefully choreographed set of movements to intimidate me, or if he might actually get angry enough to lose control. Either way, I wouldn't let the zombie get close enough for me to find out. If I had to, I'd take the thing's head off with my whip and then burn it to ash with fire magic.

But something broke inside me. I was so tired of depending on people who only had their own selfish motivations. It made me sick to think of how much of my brother's life had been wasted at the hands of people who just wanted to use him—blood-thirsty vampires, Zarella and his chaos-loving necromancers, Jacob and his epic guilt over the Manhattan disaster.

Zarella wasn't an ally. He never would be. His skills and resources were valuable, but I didn't want him involved. I'd find a way without him.

I flicked the whip, and the end of it blurred as it lashed out, slicing the zombie's pant leg but not touching skin.

Then I slumped and put on a defeated look.

"You're right," I said. "I can't do it alone. I'm not powerful enough."

"See? I knew you'd come around," the zombie said, backing off and assuming its former neutral posture. "Now, when and where will we defeat the mages?"

"Swear to me that you won't harm any innocents when the time comes," I said.

"I have absolutely no intention of it," he said. "Though I hope you do not consider the mages to be in your category of innocents."

"No, I don't." I heaved a heavy sigh. "It's going to happen at the Manhattan Rip. The mages believe it will be best to begin the process of sealing the rips at the origin. The Steins don't know I overheard them say so."

"When?"

"January thirty-first. If you care to look into it, you'll see it's a very good date for powerful magic."

I squinted at the zombie. I'd given the real date because I assumed I couldn't trick him there. He had resources at his disposal, and even though he wasn't a magic user himself, he presumably knew powerful crafters who would understand magical timing. He would probably arrive at that date as the most magically significant in the near future, just as the witches in my coven had. But as long as I could keep him from showing up at the actual location of the conflux, it wouldn't matter.

"I'm counting on you to mobilize everything you have against the mages." I said. "Will you do it?"

"With pleasure." The words seemed to slither from the zombie's lips, and it was all I could do not to writhe away.

I wasn't sure if I would fool him or not, but for the moment he seemed to have bought it.

When I'd originally messaged Zarella, I'd expected I *would* be begging for his help. Yes, he'd saved my brother in a sense, by keeping Evan hidden from Jacob and the mages for several years, but nearly at the expense of Evan's life. My brother *had* no life. He was a shell of a person, addicted to the high of vamp bites and isolated from humanity during a time when he should have been finishing high school and then going out into the world. Evan would never get that time back, and he might never be able to function normally in society. Zarella had made sure of that.

Zarella relished darkness, and I couldn't let him unleash more of it into the world. People like him and my uncle didn't deserve to be walking free. I was done with the psychopath. I needed to respect my own morals, even if it made my mission riskier and more uncertain. Even if it meant I had to burn myself out with magic and die in the process.

"You'll keep me apprised of your plans?" I asked.

"Of course," Zarella said.

I nodded and then waited, my whip in hand and magic still charging it, for the zombie to turn and leave the yard before I went back inside.

Realizing I should have done it before, I spent a few minutes creating wards around the house. I wasn't particularly skilled with them, but I knew enough to create basic ones, and since my magical ability had elevated to Level III, I actually had enough magical power to create them. I had my demon lookouts, but wards provided an extra layer of slightly different signaling, should anyone try to sneak up on me in Rogan's house. If anyone or anything approached, I could disappear into the *in-between*. Between my demons, wards, and my hellhound-doodle, I almost felt safe there.

It was late, and weariness tugged at me, but while I had the cover of darkness, I wanted to do one more thing. I needed to scout the location of the Boise Rip.

I faded to the *in-between* and used the water still puddled in the sink to transport myself to the hills near the rip, to a ravine with winter-frozen water in it.

The gray mist stirred around me, disturbed by my sudden appearance below a rolling ridge just beyond the cordoned-off site of the rip. I hiked up to the top. The interdimensional tear didn't visually register in the *in-between*, but there was a sense of something out there—an energetic disturbance. Not something you could consciously feel, but a phenomenon that sent out ripples to unnerve one's ancient, instinctual senses.

Even though it was the dead of night and completely dark in the realm of the living, the in-between had its ever-present grayish glow. It was enough light to see the contours of the hills that made up the site of the rip, which was located several miles outside of the city among the high-desert foothills.

Loki appeared beside me, and I surveyed the area, trying to guess where the mages would stage their little play. There was no place for me to hide, except maybe behind a nearby hill, but the mages wouldn't be dumb enough not to check the surroundings.

I still didn't know how Lynnette thought she and the other witches were going to help, but there was no safe place for them near the rip.

Turning to the pull of the living, I left the *in-between* so I could see the scene in full.

The sight of the rip struck me with awe for a moment. The void-black interior of the vertical slice didn't reveal anything, but even from a half mile away I could hear the crackle of the neon-blue magic that licked out around its edges like flames. The magic served to outline the rip, which at its largest pulsation point was over twenty stories tall. Even in the dark, it was impressive.

Loki whined and danced around beside me.

"Chill, boy," I whispered. "We don't want to attract attention."

By the blue light of the rip, I could just make out the road that had been carved around the site. Armored vehicles drove the circuit night and day, ready to combat anything that came through or descend on anyone who tried to trespass too close. On some of the surrounding peaks, there were heavy artillery stations set up with their cannons aimed at the rip.

How could I get close to the rip? And how could I do it before the mages showed up?

If I were more skilled with necromancy, I could control an arch-demon and ride it in. Yeah, that would work great right up to the point when the Supernatural Forces obliterated me and my ride from existence. Or, if the Steins already had the guards out of the way, the mages would do it themselves.

I cursed under my breath. The *in-between* was my best way to sneak around unseen, but I couldn't take anyone else with me into limbo land. I might be able to get close, and maybe even pop out and grab Evan, but then what? I needed a way to get him out.

My head ached with fatigue and magical drain. I needed rest. And healing. And a few well-timed strokes of brilliance.

"Let's go back to Rogan's," I whispered to Loki.

We went back to the ravine and transported to the dark house, appearing next to the sink I'd left filled with water. I kicked off my shoes and crawled into bed. For a few minutes, I thought I wouldn't be able to sleep as memories of Rogan flowed through my mind and with them a tide of sorrow and loss. But exhaustion won out, and I slept.

I awoke to the weak winter morning light and Rogan's phone buzzing on the night stand. It was Deb calling from her burner phone.

"Hey," she said. "Gina has agreed to meet you in her downtown clinic in a half hour. Can you make it?"

I sat up, pushing back my tangled hair and blinking hard, trying to shake the grogginess of sleep.

"Yeah, I can make it," I said. "But are you sure she's okay with this? I would understand if she didn't want to treat me."

"She's a healer first and foremost," Deb said. "It wouldn't be like her to deny someone in need. Plus, I told her the news reports are bogus, and she seemed open to my explanation."

"Okay," I said reluctantly. I hated the idea of dragging anyone else into my troubles, but using the *in-between*, I could go to and from her clinic without being spotted. For probably the hundredth time, I felt a swell of gratitude that Rogan had showed me how to travel through space using limbo land. "Thanks for setting it up. I'll be there."

"Lynnette wants to meet tonight instead of our usual time. I'm assuming you're free?" Her tone took on a teasing lilt.

"Gee, let me check my appointments," I said with light sarcasm. "Yep, I think I can squeeze in a coven meeting."

She gave a little giggle, and the sound of it eased some of the tightness in my chest.

"So glad to hear that. I'll get Gina to set up a glass of water and then send you a pic so you can travel straight into her clinic," she said. "And official time for the coven is five o'clock at Becky's parents' place."

"Is everything okay there at home?" I asked. "Has anyone been harassing you?"

"Nah, Roxanne and I are good," she said. But I could read in her voice that something else had happened.

"What is it?" I pressed.

"Oh, it's nothing to worry about," Deb said, the lightness in her tone still slightly forced. "The police are trying to get me to come in for questioning. Um . . . the feds, too."

"Shit," I muttered. "I'm sorry. How are you keeping them off?"

"Chris gave me some good advice about my rights," she said.

Chris? Oh right, Lagatuda, aka Tall Detective.

"You're not going to have to get a lawyer, are you?" I asked, suddenly horrified as the thought occurred to me. The absolute last thing Deb needed was more legal expenses. She was already completely tapped out, money-wise.

"Only if they try to charge me with something."

I massaged my temple. The authorities could charge her if they suspected she was helping me hide or she knew where I was.

"Well, this will all be over before it gets that far, so don't worry about that," I said, trying to sound as confident as I could.

"Yeah, it's all going to work out. Don't forget about your appointment. See you tonight."

We hung up, and I threw back the covers, got dressed, and scooted into the kitchen to make a quick pot of coffee. Loki whined and pranced, begging for food.

"Sorry, no dog chow here," I said, scratching his neck in an attempt to distract him. "You can eat when we go to the coven meeting tonight."

His whining grew more insistent, and I couldn't help a quiet laugh. Even though he was part hellhound, at times he was every bit a domesticated house pet. I opened cabinets, looking for anything that might serve as a dog snack. Finding an unopened package of beef jerky, I ripped the top off the bag. When Loki got a whiff of it, he panted up at me.

"This is a special treat," I said. "Don't expect this every day."

I tossed a piece of dried meat, and he rose up on his hind legs to snatch it out of the air. By the time I'd fed him half the bag, my coffee was ready. I had a few minutes before I had to ghost over to Gina's clinic, so I sipped the steaming brew and tuned to my necro senses, checking in with the minor demons I had posted. A few of them were around Rogan's house, and I'd also set some near my apartment.

I poked into the mind of the one posted across from the front door of the apartment Deb and I shared just in time to see a generic dark sedan pull up to the curb. Hey. I knew that car. My hand paused with the mug a few inches from my lips as I watched Detective Lagatuda get out and go to the front door.

My first instinct was to get Deb on the phone immediately. But when she opened the door and smiled brightly up at him, I stuffed my phone back in my jacket pocket. I watched with my eyes narrowed, still not completely convinced she was safe. She didn't invite him in. Or maybe she did, and he refused. She stood in the doorway and he on the front porch. Their conversation was short, and when he turned to leave, there was a goofy smile on Lagatuda's face.

I snorted an amused laugh. Aww. Tall Detective was checking on Deb. I found myself grinning in spite of myself as I rinsed out my mug and then faded to the *in-between*.

My healing session with Gina was blessedly uneventful. When I went to pay her, she held up a hand.

"Deb already gave me the fee," she said. "She wanted to make completely sure that your payment wouldn't be traced to me."

I put my bank card away, shaking my head at myself. "I'm sorry, that was really careless of me. At least someone was thinking ahead."

Gina put her hand on my arm. "Don't be so hard on yourself, Ella. You've been through the ringer in the past few months, and you're really in the thick of it now. Pace yourself, okay? I can only do so much. Some of the damage is permanent."

"I appreciate everything you've done for me," I said. "Especially now that I'm public enemy number one. Or two. I don't know. Anyway, no matter what happens, I just wanted to say thank you."

I felt a little guilty as I faded into the *in-between* because when I went up against the mages, I would undo all of Gina's skilled work. I'd do that and worse. I'd do whatever it took, and there was a good chance that when it was all over, there wouldn't be a healer in the world who could fix me.

Back at Rogan's, I let Loki out into the back yard to relieve himself, and as I watched my hellhound-doodle run around sniffing every bush and tree trunk, I considered what I'd done. I'd lied to Phillip Zarella with the hope that he'd be far, far away from Boise when the time of the conflux arrived. But would he be able to wreak havoc in Manhattan?

It was entirely possible that Zarella could stir up shit at that rip. Maybe I'd made a poor choice in trying to redirect him there. But at the very least, he wouldn't be in the vicinity where he could do my brother more harm.

I squeezed my eyes closed and pressed my fingertips into my eyelids, suddenly unsure of everything. Maybe I should have just let Zarella join us at the Boise Rip.

I sucked in a sharp breath and gave my head a shake. No, my gut told me that Zarella shouldn't be there. I had to trust that. I couldn't afford to second-guess everything. I'd drive myself nuts.

If only I had Rogan and Damien on my side. I blew out my breath slowly, trying to center myself. I couldn't dwell on what I didn't have. I had enough problems to focus on.

I used the *in-between* to pop into the desert wilderness surrounding the Boise Rip again, staying well outside the restricted zone. The hills were bare, cold, and windy, the sparse sage brush reduced to their skeletons at this time of year. On distant ridges I saw a few people here and there, some with their dogs. Hardcore trail runners who trained year-round. With Loki bounding ahead of me, I'd probably blend in with winter hikers if anyone happened to spot me.

Reaching out with my necro senses, I located a lone minor demon in a ravine, probably looking for some ice to peck through in the frozen stream there so the creature could get a sip of water. I probed into its mind, taking control of the creature and sending it into flight. Taking a lazy, circling route, I directed it closer and closer to the site of the rip.

A minor demon flying past shouldn't attract the soldiers' attention, as long as the creature didn't do anything unusual. The soldiers were concerned with the large arch-demons. Minor demons were little more than pests to the soldiers, and unless a lot of the creature flocked through the tear, Supernatural Forces usually didn't waste their high-powered weapons on the smaller pests. It would have been like taking a bazooka to a mosquito. That was what they'd say, anyway. It was one of those things they tended to gloss over because it wouldn't be received well by the public that the smaller demons were allowed to just cruise on through. But having been employed by a different but related department, I understood why they didn't bother with minor demons, and the reason was much more mundane. Everything I'd done on Demon Patrol—every house call, every kill—had resulted in paperwork. The elite Supernatural Forces didn't need to be wasting their time filling out incident reports every time they lit up one of the bat-like creatures. So they ignored them.

And I could use that to my advantage.

I sent my spy closer to the rip, looking for anything that might be useful. The armored trucks were making their usual circuit of the road around the perimeter of the restricted area. Four additional vehicles were parked in a row near the base-camp area where there was a permanent structure, presumably with a field office, bathrooms, and whatever else the soldiers needed while on shift.

I stuffed my fists in my coat pockets, tucked my chin in against the wind, and followed the nearest hiking trail away from the rip site. I'd spent enough time staring that way, and I didn't want to draw attention. Besides, I didn't need to. I had different eyes through which to scan the area, and the minor demon I'd commanded had a fine view of everything below.

I picked up a stick and threw it for Loki, and he gleefully ran off to fetch it while I watched through the eyes of the demon.

There was no way anyone could just saunter over the hills onto the site—or get away from the site, for that matter— without being seen. I had the *in-between*, but that wasn't enough. At minimum, I needed a way to get Evan out. And if Lynnette had come up with something that could truly help, I also needed a way to get a handful of witches close enough to do their work. I assumed they'd need to get close, anyway. Many magics could be casted from afar, but complicated work, and especially when under stress, needed to be in close proximity of the target.

Something in the periphery of the demon's view caught my attention. Movement. It was a new armored truck approaching. I watched as it stopped at a checkpoint and then continued on. It pulled up to the base, and half a dozen soldiers piled out of the back. I squinted, concentrating.

The soldiers went inside the building. A minute later, one of the trucks that had been patrolling the circuit pulled up, and soldiers got out of that vehicle, too. But instead of going inside, those ones went straight to the newly arrived truck and got in. The driver wheeled it around and took off back the way he'd come, crossing the checkpoint without stopping and then continuing past the restricted area and away from the site of the rip.

Shift change. There weren't any barracks at the site, so the soldiers had to rotate shifts. I wasn't sure how often it occurred, but like everything else with the elite forces, odds were good it was on a strict and regular schedule. Maybe every eight hours, was my guess.

Any time there was a shuffling-around point in a process, there was an opportunity. Was there a way to use it to get the witches near the rip?

I tried to slow my spinning thoughts. There was no point in trying to go too far with the idea before I knew what Lynnette had in mind.

I found a couple more minor demons nearby and sent one to follow the truck that was leaving the site and the other to do some fly-bys past the big gun stations set up on the hills around the rip.

I stayed a bit longer to observe, but when a stiff winter wind picked up, the cold finally drove me to take shelter. I went down into the ravine where the first demon had been looking for water and faded to the *in-between*. Limbo land felt blessedly numb compared to the hard cold of the bright Boise day. I crouched among the tangled tumbleweeds that had collected around the stream and found a bit of water. My skeletal fingers trailed the surface and took me and Loki back to Rogan's.

With a few hours until the coven meeting, I was surprised to find my mind and body powering down. Maybe it was the combination of deep healing and being out in the frigid air. Whatever the cause, I set the alarm on Rogan's phone and then fell onto the sofa and slept.

In my sleep, some part of me remained vigilant, cycling through the minor demons I'd commanded to keep an eye on the rip site. Or maybe it was my brain replaying and processing what I'd observed, it was hard to be sure.

I woke with a jolt and opened my eyes to Loki's fuzzy face filling my vision. At first I wasn't sure where I was. The phone alarm was singing a nerve-jangling tune, and the device was doing a vibrating dance over the end table. Right, Rogan's burner and Rogan's house.

Inhaling sharply, I blinked around the room and tried to clear the cobwebs of sleep. This was no time to be foggy-headed. Lynnette would be unveiling her big idea for the conflux, and we'd be casting our ballots for the coven officers.

I pushed off the sofa and Loki trotted behind me to the kitchen, where we spirited through the *in-between* to the downtown penthouse.

As I hoped, I arrived at Becky's parents' place before the others. Becky stiffened when I appeared in the corner of the living room.

She pressed a hand to her chest. "I don't know if I'll ever get used to that."

"Sorry," I said sheepishly. "I'd text you a warning, but I'm trying to stay off-grid as much as possible."

"Understandable," she said.

She was preparing a platter of olives, cheese slices, and crackers, typical coven meeting fare. On the counter behind her was a cheesecake, most likely store bought judging by its perfect edges and angles.

"How are we looking for the election?" I asked.

"No one else has come forward for the position of Keeper of Means, so I should be good there."

I leaned a hip against the edge of the counter. "Out of curiosity, what brought you to Lynnette's coven? I missed the part where you all talked about that sort of stuff. And apologies if this sounds weird, but you don't seem to have the dark edge she seemed to have sought out in most of the membership."

Deb had told me, back when Lynnette had handpicked her coven members and before she'd roped me in, that they'd spent a lot of time doing group bonding exercises. I couldn't say I was too deeply disappointed to have skipped that stage, but it meant I'd lost out on a lot of insights about the other members.

Becky gave me a shrewd, narrow-eyed look. "What, this cardigan doesn't say badass witch to you?" She plucked at the thick winter-white sweater she wore over a beige turtleneck.

I cracked a grin and snorted a laugh. "Not exactly. But that's not what I mean. It isn't about your appearance. You obviously come from a well-to-do family, to use a stodgy phrase, and that's not the pattern with most of Lynnette's recruits. Most of us are orphans, either literally or symbolically, and grew up with very little money, family support, what have you. You don't seem to fit that mold."

Damn, it felt good to say those things out loud. It struck me suddenly that there were a lot of taboo topics within the coven. Up to that point, I'd mostly thought of them as things that I shouldn't mention because I was the one member who'd been coerced into the coven. Many of the forbidden subjects had to do with Lynnette herself and the fact that most of the members were so blindly loyal to her. As I'd discovered with Deb, there was no criticizing the coven leader in certain company. But I'd never even felt it was acceptable to make such an observation about the similar demographics and backgrounds of the members.

"In that way, I don't," she said. She gave a nonchalant shrug of one shoulder. "But I've got near-mage fire magic, and it's quite rare. You know how Lynnette likes magical rarities."

My eyes widened. I hadn't known about Becky's fire talent. I easily sensed that she was a high Level II like most of the women in the coven. Occasionally a crafter had a higher aptitude with one element, or even more rare, with two.

"You're trying to feel it, aren't you?" she asked.

I nodded. "I can only sense your overall approximate aptitude."

"That's one of the perks of an elemental talent. It's undetectable, so it can stay secret if needed."

I was on the verge of asking her how Lynnette had discovered her talent when the door chimed. While Becky went to answer it, I poured Loki a bowl of dog chow and set it down on a marble tile of the kitchen floor. He dug in with enthusiasm, scattering a few kibble pieces around the dish.

I straightened to find that Lynnette and Jen had arrived. The coven leader carried a little carved wooden box under her arm.

She lofted it in both hands when she saw me looking. "For ballots," she said brightly, tucking it against her body again like it was her high-strung chihuahua rather than an inanimate object.

I gave her a thin smile but eyed the box again. Something about the way she clutched it caused a faint tightness to cascade through my gut.

The other women arrived alone or in pairs, and the overall mood was subdued with an undercurrent of anxious anticipation.

Lynnette called us to order still holding the ballot box. She ran through some minor business from previous meetings and then took a breath and scanned the faces in the room.

"We need to lay out what we're going to do at the conflux," she said, giving me a brief nod. "But first we'll do elections. This is the final step in solidifying our coven, and I for one am thrilled to have reached this point."

She turned to Jen, who had a stack of half-sheets of paper in her hand. The vampire witch rose and began distributing the sheets.

Deb began digging in her purse. "I've got some extra pencils in here. Teachers always have to carry spares."

"No writing utensils necessary," Lynnette said. "The ballots will respond to your magic. All you have to do is aim a spark at each checkbox."

I frowned and glanced around the room. Lynnette was going to try to manipulate the elections, and no one else seemed to realize it. Becky was sitting next to me on the sofa.

I shifted my weight and my elbow bumped hers. Her gaze slid over to mine, and I twitched my brows upward in question. She gave a tiny widening of her eyes. She knew something was up, too.

I looked around at the others again, watching for any signs of concern. But everyone was intent on their ballots. I lifted mine and saw the candidates' names for each position, plus lines for write-ins. Drawing the tiniest tendril of fire magic, I touched it to the box next to each person who had my vote.

As I watched Lynnette start to walk around with the box, it struck me just how desperate she'd become. She must have realized she'd lost her hold on too many of the witches if she'd stooped to this.

With the ballots all tucked into the box, Lynnette went back to her spot as the focus of the group.

"Now, as per protocol, an assistant and I will go through the ballots," she said. She took a breath to continue.

"Becky," I cut in before she could say anything more.

Lynnette's gaze swung over to me. "What?"

"I'm suggesting that Becky should assist you," I said evenly.

Lynnette's jaw clenched for a split second. Her attention shifted over to Becky.

"I'd be honored to assist," she said smoothly.

"Okay." I could tell Lynnette's mind was spinning, trying to come up with some reason to go against us. But she failed. "You all can check out the refreshments while we go through the ballots. We'll reconvene in ten."

I tried not to gloat as I watched Becky join Lynnette at the coffee table. Deb came to stand beside me, clearly somewhat keyed up about the election. She was running for Keeper of Ritual, which was second-in-command to the coven leader.

The mood of the other women seemed to have split into two or three different factions. I watched the interactions and tried to listen in but couldn't quite pinpoint which of the women were with Becky and which might be in on Lynnette's attempt at ballot fraud.

"Ella?" Deb asked, waving a hand in front of my face, her brows pinched in concern.

"Sorry," I muttered. "I just have a lot on my mind."

"Understatement of the century," she said. She touched the back of my wrist. "Have you eaten anything today?"

I passed a hand over my eyes. I'd meant to grab a bite after feeding Loki, but I'd gotten distracted talking to Becky. "No, not yet."

She turned and quickly stacked up some cheese and crackers in one hand, and then held it out at me. "Eat. After the meeting I'll go get you some takeout."

"You nervous about all this?" I asked, mechanically munching on Ritz and sharp cheddar.

"A little," she admitted in a low voice. "I really, really want the position."

"I don't think you have anything to worry about," I said.

I was fairly certain that Deb would win the vote, but almost equally certain that Lynnette wanted her opponent, Marta, to win and had intended to make that happen with her manipulations. While Deb supported and believed in our coven leader, my best friend wasn't one of Lynnette's true inner circle because if that were the case, Deb would have been involved in the scheme to harvest rip magic. She'd known nothing about it until later.

Marta, on the other hand? Her thinly-veiled imitation of Lynnette's goth-chic style made it obvious that Marta was more than a supporter. Worshipper was more like it.

Some of the conversation around the kitchen island began to die down, catching my attention. Many of the women were openly watching Lynnette and Becky. I turned around to get a full view of the seating area where we'd gathered to cast our votes.

Becky and the coven leader were exchanging quiet but obviously terse words. Lynnette's cheeks were reddening, a rare outward sign of agitation from the usually cool witch.

Jen walked a few steps toward them. "What's wrong?" she asked.

Lynnette flashed her an irate look. "Nothing, we're just trying to sort out the votes."

"Hey, Becky," I called. "Need some help counting votes?"

I strode toward the pair, my eyes on the box. Lynnette clutched it, but Becky clearly had an interest in it. Ballots were scattered in three haphazard piles on the coffee table.

Becky planted her hands on her hips. "I need help with *something* because my ballot isn't there."

"What do you mean?" I asked, stooping to scoop up the pieces of paper. Lynnette tried to go for them, but she was too slow. I quickly counted them. "This is the right number. Yours has gotta be here."

"Nope," Becky said. "I tore the lower left corner off and burned a hole in the upper right corner."

I had to suppress an appreciative smile. "Really," I said, drawing out the word.

I knelt on one knee and began laying out the ballots on the coffee table. Even though I'd seen it coming, I could barely believe Lynnette had resorted to something so . . . *silly*. It was like an episode of a really bad police and lawyer show.

The women had crowded around, watching me spread out the pieces of paper. I got to the last one and then rose and surveyed the table.

"I don't see a ballot with a tear and a burn in the corners," I said. I looked around at the faces of the other witches. "How about you guys?"

I looked over at Lynnette with raised brows. Everyone else stared at her, too.

"Well?" I asked. "Where's Becky's ballot?"

She stood there frozen for a second, and then her expression broke and she scoffed. "Obviously it's still in the box."

She flipped the latch and opened the box's lid. Before she could stick her fingers inside, I reach for my magic, drawing earth, air, and fire all at once. The fire sparked against her hands, and she let out a shrill shriek and dropped the box. I formed a little curved basket out of earth magic that caught the box before it hit the floor. A swirl of air magic pushed it over to where I stood.

I grasped the box and let my magic go. "Last chance to come clean," I said quietly.

She just stood there, her cheeks an angry red and her fists balled at her sides.

In the box, I found the real ballots. The set on the table was fake.

"This was a set-up," Lynnette hissed. "Someone tampered with the results, and they're trying to frame me."

I snorted. "Really? You think someone framed you? That's just ... well, it's sad. You used to be a lot better at manipulating the coven. This has got to be your most pathetic scheme yet. I almost feel sorry this is how you got caught. It's like when they caught the Son of Sam killer on a parking ticket."

I could easily tell, looking around the faces of the coven members, which ones had been in on Lynnette's failed trick. Marta looked alternately sick to her stomach and defiant. Elena's eyes were darting toward the door like she was ready to make a break for it. And Jen just looked resigned and much too calm, which could only mean that the big revelation was no surprise to her.

Adriana, a quiet witch whose dark eyes were flashing as she folded her arms, had to be one of Becky's affiliates. She and Becky had identical triumphant expressions.

I heard a tiny sound of distress that made me turn. Deb. Her eyes were filling with tears and her expression was a mess of anger warring with sadness.

I started to go to her, but she didn't even see me. Her attention was trained on Lynnette. My best friend slowly stood.

"How could I be so stupid?" Deb whispered. The tears spilled over her lower lids and trickled down her cheeks. She walked toward Lynnette and stood facing the coven leader. "How could I be so stupid *again*? Why do I choose to align myself with such awful, selfish, manipulative people? Keith . . . you. What the hell is wrong with me?"

My heart nearly ripped in two. Any satisfaction I'd felt dissolved into grief for my best friend. She blamed herself for giving her loyalty to her stupid, loser ex-husband and this manipulative witch.

"It's not you, Deb," Becky said. "Trust me, it's not you. Lynnette's spent a lifetime learning how to control people. We all got sucked in, otherwise we wouldn't have ended up here."

I cast Becky a grateful look, hoping the words would have an impact on Deb.

"Not everyone got sucked in," Deb said. She turned around, her eyes finding mine. "You didn't. You knew. You tried to tell me, but I wouldn't listen."

I opened my mouth to respond but didn't get the chance.

"Ladies," Lynnette cut in. She'd put on a placating expression and a tone to match. Words began sliding smoothly from her lips. I knew even without feeling it that she was on the verge of trying to pull power to employ her verbal magic. "You're all being a bit dramatic, don't you think? It was a mistake. A stupid one. Don't get carried away. Come on, we can work this out, you guys."

I saw Deb's face harden a split second before she whirled on Lynnette. "Sit down and shut up," Deb roared.

Lynnette blinked and jumped as if she'd been struck. Everyone else in the room stiffened, too, me included.

Deb pointed to the nearest easy chair. She put on her take-no-nonsense teacher face. "Don't make me ask again. And if you reach for your magic, I will have Ella fry your brain and cut you off from your magic forever. She's a Level III now, in case you forgot. She can do it."

I had no idea if my newfound power included the ability to fry a human brain, but in that moment, I kind of believed Deb. Lynnette must have, too, because she obediently went to the chair and perched on the edge of it with her fingers woven together in her lap.

Deb turned to the rest of us. "Now. Becky and Ella will go through the ballots and—*hey!*"

I followed Deb's gaze to Elena, who had stood and started edging toward the door while we were all distracted by Deb's showdown with Lynnette.

Pulling earth power, I formed a wall of green that blocked the front door and then turned to Deb and lifted my hand. "You were saying?"

She gave me a sharp nod. "Yes. Thank you. I was saying that Becky and Ella will go through the real ballots. Then we'll talk about who actually won and what we're going to do about Lynnette, Marta, Elena, and Jen."

On the last name, Deb's voice and face fell as it seemed to hit home that Jen had been in on Lynnette's schemes. Deb had considered Jen a close friend. At times I'd wondered whether Jen might be an ally, but I wouldn't have guessed that the vampire witch was so deeply involved in the coven leader's nefarious activities. My heart gripped again for Deb and the hurt she was surely feeling. This was a hell of a lot of disappointment to deal with.

I released Elena from the web of earth magic, and then Becky and I took the box and all the papers over to the kitchen island and began going through the ballots. We discovered Deb had been elected Keeper of Ritual, according to the true vote.

"Hey," I said to Becky in a low voice. "Lynnette and her minions didn't elect anyone for Keeper of Means. Don't you think that's weird?"

She frowned at the ballots and then looked up at me. "Yeah . . . except in the fake ballots, you won. I edged you out by one vote in the real ballots."

"Huh?"

"Even though you withdrew, they wrote in your name on the fake ballots. You also got write-in votes on the real ballots."

I blinked. "That doesn't make sense."

She gave me a wry smile. "What, you're not used to being one of the popular girls?"

I barked a laugh. "Um, no. But I don't think that's what's going on here."

"The witches like you," she said. "I think even Lynnette's do, too. You saved them. You may not want to be here, but you're well-regarded."

I shook my head. I wasn't buying it. Lynnette wouldn't want me to be the Keeper of Means. Why would she make me the winner on the fake ballots? She probably hadn't wanted Becky to take the position, either, but why was she okay with me winning? An idea occurred to me. "After we're done, can I take all the ballots? Just for a while."

Becky's manicured brows shot up. "Sure, I guess. As long as you bring them back. We should probably keep them in our records."

"I'm happy you won Keeper of Means," I said. "You're obviously better suited to digging up the dirt in the financials, and I'm going to be a little preoccupied for a while anyway."

Her hands stilled, and her eyes met mine. "Oh, damn. Lynnette had an idea about something we could do for you at the conflux. We should have waited to out her."

I shook my head. "No, it's okay. I had my doubts about her intentions. I think odds are pretty low she was actually going to help."

"Maybe," Becky said. "But you can't go in there alone. I'm sure the others will be willing to help. You can count me in. Just tell us what you want us to do."

I gave her a grateful look, but there was one problem. I hadn't figured out how I could utilize anyone else.

"Thanks," I said. "Let's just get through this."

We rejoined the group, where Deb had Marta, Jen, and Elena on the floor next to Lynnette's chair. They were sitting cross-legged with nearly identical unhappy expressions, like grade-schoolers who'd been caught bullying a kid at recess.

"Deb was legitimately elected Keeper of Ritual," Becky said without preamble.

Everyone except Lynnette and her buddies let out a cheer.

"I was legitimately elected Keeper of Means, by only one vote in the real ballots. I lost to Ella in the fake ballots," Becky continued. "And Jen was the sole nominee for Keeper of Records, so she won."

"Clearly Jen's position isn't going to stand," Adriana said. "In fact, I move that those four get kicked out of the coven as soon as possible."

Everyone started talking at once, and then Lynnette shouted above the din.

"That's not possible," she said. "As founder, I can't be removed."

"Then we'll have to dissolve the organization," Adriana said.

Deb held a hand high, silencing the arguments. "What we'll *do* is look into all options, think about it, and then decide. For now, we need a formal vote to take Lynnette out of decision-making capacity. And you should know that as long as she has no authority, by the charter rules as Keeper of Ritual I'll be filling in for her. We also need a vote to suspend all four of them until we can decide what to do."

"I move to do that," Adriana said, her anger still clear.

"Second," several of us chimed in at once.

We voted, and as expected there were only four dissenters.

"They shouldn't have even been allowed to vote," someone muttered not-so-subtly.

"That may be true, but at least we know the decision was legitimately arrived at," Deb said firmly.

I watched her with admiration. Even while still reeling from the emotional gut-punches of learning her leader and friends were frauds, she'd immediately stepped in to fill the leadership void. It was obvious the women respected her. Well, the ones whose respect actually meant anything. Deb was going to be an amazing mom. And a hell of a leader.

"What are we going to do about *them*?" Becky asked, tipping her head at Lynnette and the others.

"No one leaves here until Lynnette gives the new officers full access to all of the coven's records," Deb said.

"But Jen was elected Keeper of Records," I pointed out. "We can't let that stand."

Deb sighed. "You're right. She's officially suspended. Can I get a volunteer to fill in?"

Adriana's hand shot up, and Deb nodded at her.

Becky had gone to the kitchen for her bag. She returned holding a tablet in one hand and crooking the index finger of her other hand at Lynnette. "I need all accounts and passwords."

Lynnette looked like she was ready to vomit as she shakily stood, smoothed her hands down the front of her off-the-shoulder t-shirt, and then trudged toward the new Keeper of Means as if going to her own execution.

Jen was the only one who had actually looked remorseful. Silent tears had started spilling down her round cheeks while Deb was talking, and then the vampire witch held her face in her hands, her shoulders shaking as she cried.

I couldn't help a small stab of sympathy. Her life hadn't been easy, but she'd finally found some peace in the vampire community, where she lived in her little bachelorette pad, and with the coven, which had given her a place to belong among people who didn't care that she was a vamp. She'd come to my aid a number of times, and I'd genuinely liked her.

Unexpected sadness gripped me as all that had just gone down really began to sink in. We'd obliterated the coven and in the process also shattered the future, security, sisterhood, and family it had represented for most of the women in it. No one knew exactly how the pieces would fall, but nothing would ever be the same. Most likely, the coven would have to be dissolved. It was going to be hard on everyone, emotionally and financially.

I sidled over to Deb while the others moved away from the three pariahs still sitting on the floor. Whispered conversations started up among the women who were still in good standing.

"What *are* we going to do with the four of them?" I whispered.

"Nothing," she said. "It's not like we can lock them up. The best we can do is make sure they can't steal from the coffers, lock us out of any accounts, or delete anything important. But we're not jailers. We'll have to let them go. I suspect that may be the last we see of Marta and Elena. Lynnette might still try to get something out of us, though."

"And what about Jen?"

Deb heaved a weighty sigh and looked over at the vampire witch, who was still sobbing into her hands.

"I don't want to make too many assumptions," she said carefully. "But Jen may be . . . salvageable. I don't think all of this was really her. Maybe Lynnette even used verbal magic to coerce her."

"You mean you'd pull for letting Jen stay?" I asked incredulously.

She gave a tiny shrug. "That depends on her, how badly she wants it, and what she's willing to do to show it. And what everyone else thinks, of course. But we'll worry about that later. Who knows if we'll even have a coven anymore, after it's all said and done."

After another fifteen minutes or so, Becky seemed satisfied she'd gotten enough information out of Lynnette. She carried her tablet over to me and Deb.

"We might as well dismiss them," Becky said. "If the others are willing to stay, we can talk about what's next."

Deb nodded. She went over and sat in the chair Lynnette had vacated and touched Jen's shoulder. The vampire witch lifted her tearstained face. Deb spoke quietly to her, and a fresh wave of tears filled Jen's eyes. She made a brief reply and then stood up and went to gather her things.

Deb rose with her hands pressed into her lower back. This was a lot more stress and strain than I wanted her to experience at this point in her pregnancy, and I could tell she was physically exhausted and mentally drained. But the others seemed expectant, and Becky was right—we needed to at least start talking about how we were going to move forward.

"Before we let the four of you go," Deb said. "I'd like to hear what Lynnette wanted to do at the conflux." She turned to the former leader of the coven. "If you want any hope of getting back in our good graces and avoiding criminal charges, it'd be a good idea to tell us in detail how you planned to help Ella."

Criminal charges? Maybe Detective Lagatuda's influence was rubbing off more than I'd realized. Or perhaps Deb was just bluffing.

Lynnette folded her arms, and her dark red lips pressed together in the faintest of grim smiles. "In exchange for what, specifically?" she asked. "I've done nothing of a criminal nature, so your threat isn't very compelling."

I shook my head in disbelief. After everything, she thought she was still in a position to bargain? Or maybe I'd been right, and she'd never intended to help in the first place.

"You just lost your chance," Deb said. She swung her arm out and pointed at the front door. "Leave now."

Lynnette blinked twice, dropped her arms to her sides, stormed across the room, and left.

Deb faced the other three outcasts. "Did Lynnette tell any of you about her grand scheme?" she asked.

Marta and Elena sat there with stony stares. After a long pause, Jen shook her head.

"Fine," Deb said. "You three go, too."

We all watched in silence as they gathered up their things and walked out.

The nine of us who were left seemed mostly stunned and drained.

"Are we going to lose everything?" asked Latrice, one of the youngest of the group, in a small voice.

"Not if I can help it," Deb said. She sank to a chair and looked around at us. "What do we want? Do we want to try to salvage the coven?"

"I do," Latrice said.

Several more added their agreement.

Deb took a deep breath. "Okay, I'll look into whether we could make that happen. I don't think there's much more we can do tonight, though, in the way of decisions. Whatever we do, it's going to take some time. I know it's going to be hard to go back home and try to pick up the pieces, but we have each other. If you need to talk, call somebody. Okay? You're not alone in this."

The women nodded, looking weary and sad. I felt shades of the emotions I saw around me, but mostly I was incredibly proud of Deb. I knew she was amazing, but it was as if, in the middle of a crisis, she'd come alive. And right then, I knew she was meant to lead a coven. Whatever happened next, she'd be at the helm, and it would be awesome.

But for the moment, the air was heavy with devastation. And my own problems began descending once again upon me, weighing me down and filling me with equal parts determination and dread.

As the women made movements to depart and exchanged last hugs and encouraging words, I tried to take inspiration from my best friend. I had only a couple more days until the conflux.

"I know it's late," I said to Deb in a low voice. "But I need to have Roxanne look at the ballots. I want to see if she can read anything on them, any intention or anything. It just doesn't make any sense that Lynnette set me up to be the write-in winner for Keeper of Means."

Deb frowned. "You're right. That doesn't make sense at all. You're the last person Lynnette would want holding an office in the coven."

"Gee, you don't have to rub it in," I said wryly.

She gave me a faint, tired smile. "I'm just concerned."

"Me too," I said. "Lynnette doesn't do these things without a motive. Even though she's all but ousted, I have a bad feeling about this."

"Roxanne has tomorrow off from school, so I bet she's still up," Deb said. "Meet me back home?"

I gave her the stack of ballots. "See you there," I said.

I called Loki and went over to the sink. I filled a bowl with water, faded into the *in-between*, and ghosted to my apartment.

Roxanne had a special skill that I'd never even heard of before I'd met her. She could "read" objects and know who had handled or manipulated them. She'd learned the same with spells—she seemed to be able to sense who had cast magic on an object. The skill seemed to be strongest when someone she knew had touched or magicked something. If it were a stranger, she could sometimes give a bit of description.

In the months I'd known her, she'd been working hard to expand the talent. Intent was one aspect she'd been trying to hone. I hoped that her familiarity with the women in the coven would make it easier to read such information on the ballots.

I popped into the apartment's tiny kitchen. Roxanne was on the sofa watching TV. She straightened when I walked in but didn't look alarmed.

"Deb said someone would be showing up suddenly," she said. "I figured it was you, even though she didn't say."

She extracted herself from a pile of blankets and pillows and trotted across the room to give me a hug.

"That's pure crap they're saying about you," she said when she pulled back. She flipped her middle finger at the TV. "Evil media overlords."

I gave her a tired grin. "Your loyalty means a lot. But if anyone finds out you saw me, you'd get in a load of trouble, and I don't want any of this, uh, *crap* to affect you."

"No one will ever know." She mimed zipping her lips closed, locking them, and tossing the key over her shoulder.

"Wait, I'm not saying you should *lie*," I said.

"I know," she said. "Don't worry about me. I'll just make sure I'm not in a position to get asked about you in the first place. And even if by some chance I fail at that, it'll be fine. Trust me."

I gave her a shrewd look, and she raised her brows innocently. I cracked a grin. Roxanne was still a child, but she was probably right about not worrying about her. She knew how to take care of herself.

Loki appeared in the spot where I'd arrived, and Roxanne let out a delighted little shriek. The hellhound-doodle bounded to her, and they made an adorable display of greeting each other.

She was taller than I remembered but still looked like she was drowning in one of her signature oversized hoodies. I hated to think of how the coven drama would affect her. The witches had become a second family to Roxanne, and she'd been apprenticing with several of them to learn new magic skills. Deb was Roxanne's mentor, so the girl wouldn't lose that relationship, at least.

A few minutes later, Deb arrived home. She looked absolutely wiped out.

I took the stack of ballots from her.

"Deb, what's wrong?" Roxanne asked with alarm.

"It's a long story," she said. Her eyes flicked to mine. "We'll have to talk about it tomorrow."

Roxanne turned to me, accusing. "What is it?" she demanded.

Deb and I traded another look. "Let's let Deb get to bed, and I'll give you the short version. But first, I need your magical detective skills." I held up the ballots.

I knew Deb was trying to protect Roxanne, but the girl was going to find out about the coven soon enough. I would tell her only what she needed to know.

"Get," I said, shooing Deb toward the bedroom. "Sleep. We'll talk tomorrow."

She dragged herself into the room, and a minute later the strip of light under the door went dark. Deb had to be truly exhausted to skip brushing her teeth and washing her face. Poor thing. I hated to think of the strain she was under. First the horror show with me, and then the coven imploding. She needed some peace and quiet.

I flipped through the ballots and found they were still divided into the two groups—real ones and falsified ones.

I separated them, folded the stack of real ones in half, and shoved those into a back pocket of my jeans. Then I quickly sorted out the ones that had me as the write-in vote for Keeper of Means. I really only needed Roxanne's read on those ones.

"Okay," I said, beckoning Roxanne to join me on the sofa. "I know you've been working on reading the intent of the person who handled or magicked an object. Do you think you can try that on these pieces of paper?"

She looked down at them curiously. I'd turned the stack of fake ballots face down. I didn't want her distracted by what was on the papers.

"Yeah, I'll try."

"Okay, one at a time, go through them and tell me who you think had the strongest influence on each piece of paper, and their intent, if you can read that."

I held out the first one, and I felt her draw magic even before she touched it. She closed her eyes in concentration. Fine filaments of blue air magic spun around her hands and the ballot.

"Several people handled this," she said. "Women in the coven. But Lynnette's signature is the strongest."

Roxanne's brow furrowed. She cocked her head as if listening to something far off.

"Her intention is . . . yuck," she said and made a sour face. Her eyes popped open. "Lynnette intended harm with this.

Or, no, that's not quite right. She didn't intend harm with *this* literally, but she expected harm. Hoped for it."

My stomach tightened, though I wasn't surprised.

"Harm to who?" I asked, already fairly sure of the answer.

The corners of Roxanne's mouth turned down. "You."

She began to look seriously upset. I placed my hand over hers.

"I know this is kind of awful, but I really need you to do a couple more if you can," I said quietly.

"Why would Lynnette hurt you? Does this have something to do with the stuff Deb didn't want to tell me?"

I nodded. "It's related. Do you think you can read some more?"

Her unhappiness was clouding into the start of anger. "What did she do to you?"

I leaned forward. "Nothing. She didn't hurt me. But you can help me understand what she had in mind. It's really, really important."

Roxanne took a breath, clearly trying to re-center herself. She wouldn't be able to read the ballots if she got too upset. She placed the ballot on the coffee table and took the next one from the top of the stack.

"Same thing, several witches handled this paper," she said. "And it has the same icky signature. Lynnette manipulated this while thinking about something bad happening to you. I think . . . I think she expected you to *die*."

Roxanne's big eyes began to fill with tears.

"Okay, that's all I need," I said, quickly deciding not to force her to handle any more ballots. "I'm sorry that was so hard."

I reached over and pulled her into a hug.

"You have to tell me," she said, her words muffled against my shoulder. She pulled back. "You have to tell me what happened tonight with the coven."

I smothered a sigh, suddenly wishing I had Deb there. She was naturally maternal. She'd know how to deliver the bad news in the right way and how to comfort Roxanne afterward. I took a deep breath and looked into Roxanne's round eyes.

"It turns out Lynnette and a few of the other witches tried to falsify ballots for the officer elections," I said. "It was a seriously bad thing to do. Lynnette and those women won't be able to stay in the coven."

Roxanne pressed her fingers to her lips for a second. "Who are the others?"

I gave her the names.

She shook her head. "But why?"

"Well, we don't have all the answers yet, but we're pretty sure Lynnette has been trying to hide some things from the rest of us. Some of it has to do with money, we think. We don't know what else."

Her shock was fading into worry, and her eyes filled again. "What's going to happen to the coven? Are you going to split up?"

"I don't think anyone wants that, but we'll have to figure it out," I said. "No matter what, the witches still love you and we're all here for you. Deb and I aren't going anywhere, and I'm sure I can say the same for the rest of the remaining members. Okay?"

She blinked and gave a faint nod. She stared at a spot on the floor for a long moment.

"Lynnette is a bad person," she said and slumped dejectedly.

I couldn't disagree. "Why do you say that?"

"She just *is*. I could feel that something was off with her, but I didn't want to believe it because she seemed so dedicated to the coven. To all of you. How could she be such a traitor?"

"Lynnette cares more about power than anything else," I said, deciding to be frank with Roxanne. She'd had plenty of people let her down in her life, and I hated to add to the list even if it wasn't me specifically, but trying to hide the truth wasn't going to help her. "She saw the coven as a way to gain greater power. That doesn't mean she didn't care about the witches. I think she did want all of us to benefit from the coven's success, too. It's just that power was the most important thing to her."

"Yeah, I can see that now," Roxanne said, her voice tiny. "It sucks. It really, really sucks."

Tears spilled over her lower lids and ran down her cheeks. I wrapped my arms around her again.

"I know," I said. "And I'm sorry."

We sat there for nearly a minute, and I listened to her quiet crying and thought about how unfair it was. Roxanne had been abandoned by her parents years ago, her flaky brother had moved a thousand miles away for work, and now some of the women she'd looked up to and trusted had turned out to be traitors. It really, really did suck.

She sat back and wiped her cheeks. "Sometimes it seems like you can't absolutely count on anything, you know?"

"Yeah, I know it can seem that way," I said. "I've been let down by people, too. So has Deb. But you know what that makes you do? Really, really appreciate the people you *can* depend on. They're like gold."

She considered that for a couple of seconds.

"Better than gold. They're like . . . what's the rarest thing? I don't know. Platinum. I think that's more rare than gold. Yeah. You and Deb are my platinum people." She gave me a fierce look and waggled her index finger in an admonishing gesture. "Don't you dare make me demote you to, like, aluminum or something you can find everywhere. Aluminum is that crap friend who won't even write back when you text."

"I solemnly swear that I will always be one of your platinum people," I said seriously.

That actually seemed to give her a bit of ease. She took a deep breath and nodded, and then she gave me a watery little smile.

"It's late," I said. "You should get some sleep."

"Are you staying?"

"I'd like to, but I shouldn't." I shrugged. "I'm still a fugitive, and I've already put you guys at risk."

She gave me a glum nod.

"This will all be over soon, okay? Hang in there," I said.

One more hug, and then she went to the bathroom to brush her teeth and wash her face.

Loki and I slipped into the kitchen, where I ran some water in the sink and then melted from the realm of the living into the *in-between*. We traveled back to Rogan's, where I wearily fell into the easy chair and stared into the dark.

So. Lynnette had most likely expected me to die at the conflux, and that was why she'd wanted me to win the election for Keeper of Means. I wouldn't have enough time to dig into the records, and getting me out of the picture would give her plenty of additional time to figure her shit out before putting someone else in the position. She must have done something really bad with the coven's money to stoop to such an extreme. But I knew Lynnette, and she wasn't the type to just stand by and hope the mages killed me. She'd said she had a plan to help me save my brother from the mages, but that was bullshit. No, she'd wanted to be there so she could make sure I didn't make it out.

When had the tipping point happened? What exactly had turned her from wanting me in the coven badly enough to coerce me against my will to planning my death?

Maybe it was when she'd had to give up her exorcism talent to the oracle. That was her most coveted skill, the one she'd made her career and reputation on. But my guess was that the switch flipped when I became a Level III. It made me the most powerful witch in the coven, and far more powerful than she could ever dream to be. With Lynnette, it always came back to power. Perhaps she thought she'd lose her authority with the other women. Or maybe she just couldn't stand to have a witch in her coven who could wield so much more magic than she could.

I supposed I didn't have to worry about her showing up at the conflux and trying to get me killed. She was done for, as far as the coven was concerned. We had access to all the records, Becky had changed all the passwords, and Lynnette was out for good.

I fell asleep sitting in the chair and dreamed reaper dreams of roaming the *in-between* in eternal gray and silence. Eventually my dreams turned to the coven and Lynnette.

When I awoke to sunlight forcing its way through the living room curtains, I sat straight up. Something had occurred to me while I was asleep. It had seemed very, very important. I exhaled slowly through my mouth and closed my eyes, trying to bring the thought back to the surface before it disappeared into the fading memories of the night's dreams.

My brain had been chugging hard while I slept, trying to make connections.

I reached for Rogan's phone and texted Deb for Becky's number. She picked up on the first ring.

"Hey, I was just about to get your number from Deb," Becky said.

"Let me guess. You found something in the records that has to do with me. Maybe something to do with my brother?"

There was a second of silence. "How did you know?"

I let out a short, humorless laugh. "Moment of clarity."

"Are you sitting down?" she asked. "'Cause you'll want to take a seat before I tell you what I discovered."

My stomach was already winding itself into a hard ball.

"I'm sitting down," I said. "Shoot."

"I believe lynnette took a bribe from the mages, or perhaps Jacob Gregori working in concert with the mages," Becky said.

I gripped the phone hard against my ear. "A bribe for what?" I asked, but I already had an inkling.

"Well, it's like it's spelled out in a memo attached to the deposit, but—" She cut off, clearly not happy about what she was going to say next. "Didn't Damien take Evan from Lynnette's house?"

My breath stilled.

"Yes," I said after a long pause. "I broke him out of the Gregori Industries campus, and Lynnette was there with a getaway car. We took Evan to her place, and Damien ghosted my brother right out of the guest room."

"I imagine she was the one to initiate contact with whoever gave her the payment," Becky said quietly. "My guess is she offered up your brother's whereabouts."

"How much financial trouble was she in?" I asked.

"She was lying about the coven's income, and there were some large expenditures that she never told us about. I'm not sure what they were for yet."

"What about the supposed angel investor?"

Lynnette had distracted the witches from my attempt to force her to confess some of the awful things she'd done by producing a letter from an anonymous donor who was offering large sums of money to fund the coven's early days. It had worked, taking the focus off her and giving the women a reason to believe the coven would be financially viable. Most covens failed in their first few years, and every woman in our coven had a lot riding on the success of the organization.

"I can't prove it definitively, but I don't think there was one," Becky said. "There are a few regular deposits of what I believe is the bribe money, and I think she made up the story about the anonymous investor and planned to make it look like the bribe money was investor donations."

My head was starting to hurt. "So Lynnette sold out me and my brother. She's the one who told the mages where Evan was. She's the reason the mages were able to steal him away from me."

"I believe that's the case," Becky said.

Maybe I should have felt angrier, but mostly there was just hollow clarity.

Becky told me a few other things she was looking into, and then we ended the call.

I slowly got up, stiff from spending the night in a sitting position. Loki was whining to be let out, but it was broad daylight. If the neighbors saw a strange dog in the yard of a house that had seemed abandoned, there wasn't a whole lot I could do about it. I crouched down, out of view of any of the windows, and opened the back door for him.

Sitting against the wall while I waited for Loki to do his business, I pulled my knees up, hugging them to my body, and propped my chin on one kneecap.

The conflux was less than two days away. I didn't really have a plan. I didn't know what else to do to prepare.

Everything in me was pulling to try to do it on my own, but the oracle's—Switchboard's—voice echoed in my head. Going solo would lead to failure. The witches had offered to help. But what good was the comparatively feeble power of a handful of mid-level crafters against the most powerful mages in the world?

I pulled out Rogan's phone and texted Deb.

Does collective magic still work when we don't have a full coven of witches?

Female crafters had the ability to combine their power into group magic, and I'd seen it in action with my own coven. Collective magic was powerful, resulting in greater power than the sum of the individuals, but it wasn't mage-level. Still, if it were an option, it might be my best bet.

Deb replied a couple of minutes later.

It should be possible, among women who have gone through a bonding ceremony. It wouldn't be as spectacular as a full bonded coven's collective magic, but the remaining witches should be able to get a little boost, if that's what you're thinking. Is that what you're thinking? Because if so, we're all in. We've already talked about it.

My thumbs hovered over the keyboard on the phone's screen as I wavered. I hated the thought of putting the witches, and especially Deb, in the mages' crosshairs. It made me nauseous to even think about it. But I forced myself to a reply.

Yeah. I need you guys. I hate to put you in danger, but I can't do this alone. I need you to help me get Evan away from the mages. I can disappear into limbo land, but I can't take him there with me.

Remembering what I saw at the site of the Boise Rip, suddenly I knew what I needed to do.

Deb texted back: *What's the plan?*

My breath was coming a little faster as my idea took shape and my pulse sped.

I'll let you know later tonight.

I stuffed my phone in my pocket, let Loki in, and disappeared us into the *in-between*. I used limbo land to go to a spot near my old headquarters downtown, the building where I'd checked in for my Demon Patrol shifts for so many years. It was also the place where the elite Supernatural

Forces was headquartered, though in a different wing of the building than Demon Patrol.

An in the nearby parking structure, I knew I'd find Demon Patrol cars. More importantly, I'd find armored trucks. Just like the ones that patrolled the Boise Rip. I no longer had my work ID that would have gotten me into the garage, but that didn't matter. I could use the *in-between*.

First, I popped into the realm of the living outside the parking structure, across the street next to an office building I knew well. I made sure to place myself behind the large sign angled on one corner. There would be people around, but I just needed a quick glimpse of the parking garage to make sure I could get what I needed.

I faded back into limbo land and stepped out from behind the sign and into the swirling mist. Loki and I loped across the street and straight into the garage. I sensed the nearby souls of the living—guards in the booth of the garage, and others walking past or going about their work. But in limbo land, I had the parking structure to myself.

We walked up the ramp and circled up the gentle incline. A couple of times we moved out of the way of ghostly vehicles coming or going. On the third floor, we found what I wanted. The armored trucks.

I popped out of the *in-between* to rattle some truck doors, but of course found all of them locked. That was okay.

I mostly needed to get a look at the situation. I was going to come back later when there were fewer people around.

The darkly tinted glass panes of the truck's cab didn't exist in limbo land, and I knew it would be a push-button ignition that didn't require a key. Perfect. I could climb in easily and then pop into the living realm and take off with the truck.

Next, I needed to swipe a uniform. Most of the witches could hide in the back, but the driver would need to look legit to get on the rip site. I went back to the main entrance of headquarters, stood in the gray mist until the door opened, and then piggybacked inside on someone's ID swipe. Loki and I jogged through the corridors of the elite forces wing until I got to where I knew I'd find the uniform racks just inside the women's locker room.

I walked past them to a bathroom stall, where I popped into the living realm. I waited until the sounds of voices and movement died away, and then stole out of the stall to the racks. Quickly flipping through the uniforms, I took two of different sizes, just to cover my bases. Back in the bathroom stall, I pulled on the uniforms over my clothes. Fortunately, they were cut in a roomy style similar to the garb I'd seen on the news in clips of marines deployed to desert areas. These uniforms were medium gray instead of khaki.

I couldn't button and zip everything, but I didn't think it would matter. Things I wore or carried in pockets seemed to move just fine from the living realm, through the *in-between*, and back again, but I couldn't carry objects in my hands in my transitions between realms.

I had to wait while a few women came in and out, and when it was quiet once again, I filled one of the sinks, faded to the *in-between* with my triple layered clothing, and used the trick of the water to get back to Rogan's. There, I peeled off the uniforms and folded them into a pile. Then I called Deb.

"How would you and the other witches like to be in charge of Evan's getaway car?" I asked.

"Of course we will," she said almost before I'd even stopped speaking.

"You could get in a whole lot of trouble. Not to mention, you know, die at the hands of the mages."

Part of me really wanted her to back out. But I knew she wouldn't. And I knew I couldn't save Evan without her.

She scoffed. "Is that the best you've got? Walk in the park."

A faint smile almost stretched my lips, but it was too serious. I couldn't joke around.

"I'm going to steal a Supernatural Forces truck," I said. "I'll call you later tonight and let you know where to find the truck and what to do, okay?"

"Got it," she said. "We're going to stop them, Ella. We *are*."

"Okay," was all I could manage.

"Love you."

"Love you, too," I echoed.

I waited until well after sundown, put on all the clothes again, and then went downtown via the *in-between*. Getting the truck out turned out to be a fairly simple matter. Like before, I walked into the parking garage. Loki and I found a truck for the taking on the second floor, and we hopped up on the hood and shimmied through the pane-less windshield and into the cab. Then I transitioned back to the realm of the living.

I had a few minutes before a fresh shift of soldiers would head out from headquarters toward the rip. I started the engine. Loki appeared on the seat next to me, looking at me expectantly with his tongue out.

Two trucks came growling down from upper levels, and I waited until they'd gone by before pulling out and quickly catching up. The windows were so darkly tinted and the garage so dim, there was no way the soldiers could identify me. No one tried to stop us as the three trucks rolled out. I purposely slowed, letting the other two go through a light. Stopped at a red, I waited until the trucks were out of sight and then put on my signal.

I hadn't been sure where to hide the truck until a I had a stroke of genius earlier in the day. Lynnette's garage. I had the code from previous functions at her house. If she were there, she wouldn't dare come out and try to stop me from parking the truck. And if she'd fled, I didn't have to worry anyway.

Either way, if someone happened to find it, the stolen truck wouldn't get traced back to me.

When I got to Lynnette's Victorian style house and went around to the alley where the garage entrance was, I found her white SUV was gone. I pulled in, killed the engine, and then peeled off the uniform clothing and left it in the front seat.

I stood outside with Loki for a moment looking into Lynnette's courtyard, where I'd taken the oath to join the coven. I watched the windows, thinking perhaps she was hiding out in there somewhere even though her car was gone. But there was no flicker of movement. The house even felt silent and empty, somehow. Maybe she would sell it and slip away to some other place where she could once again start gathering admirers and collecting power.

Loki and I ghosted back to Rogan's, where I called Deb and told her where the truck was.

"If you and the other witches can use collective magic to your advantage, do it," I said. "But I don't think I'll be able to join in. I'll have to disappear into the *in-between* as soon as I get Evan away from the mages."

"I expected as much," Deb said.

"I'm going to check on the rip site and see if there's any sign of the Steins," I said. "If you all can gather somewhere, that might be best. You're going to have to move out really fast as soon as something pops at the rip."

"I've got a plan, don't worry," she said. "Just do what you need to do."

"Okay, we'll talk soon."

We hung up.

We didn't know the exact timing of the conflux. It could happen after about three in the morning or any time until about midnight the following night. I expected the mages would want to use the cover of darkness rather than try to carry out their plan in broad daylight. Or maybe that wasn't the sort of thing that mattered to them. The Steins were supremely entitled. They probably wouldn't feel the need to hide.

I found a long, heavy jacket of Logan's, put it on, and then used the *in-between* to go to the puddle in the ravine just beyond the restricted zone of the Boise Rip. Loki and I hiked up to a ridge, and I wrapped the coat tightly around me and sat down on the packed dirt facing the rip. He sat next to me, alert like a sentry.

I had no idea what to expect. Would the Steins float down like angels from the sky with Evan? Would they have gotten permission to come onto the site and arrive with a Supernatural Forces escort?

I nearly nodded off as the cold and lack of activity at the site began to lull me. A soft whine from Loki sharpened my attention. Someone had arrived. On another ridge outside the restricted zone, a van had pulled up. Two people had gotten out, and they were maneuvering equipment around.

I used my necro senses to catch one of my circling demon spies and send it over to the newcomers. Through its eyes, I saw that it was a news van and two men were setting up what looked like broadcasting equipment.

My heart punched against my ribcage. It was starting. And it looked like the mages wanted the world to see the whole thing.

Another van showed up shortly after the first. And then three more.

By the neon blue light of the rip, I watched the armored vehicles below, still tracing their patrol circles around the perimeter of the site. Would the mages force the soldiers to clear out? Unlikely. Supernatural Forces was there to help protect the public from ripspawn. They didn't report to the Order of Mages. Plus, the mages would want everything to look above-board. They'd allow the soldiers to remain and continue securing the site, and probably wanted the guards there so their lofty mage minds didn't have to get distracted by keeping the riffraff off the site.

But the mages wanted it all captured and broadcast. They intended to put on a show.

I pulled out Rogan's phone and called Deb.

"The mages aren't here yet, but something's happening," I said. "News crews have arrived. I think you guys better get into position. Wait until the mages arrive, though. I think we'll have time while they stage their play. If you can join some other trucks coming onto the site, do that. If not, just roll in like you belong."

"How close should we try to get?" Deb asked.

"The closer the better," I said. "But hang back enough so you don't stick out."

"We haven't talked about where we should take Evan," Deb said.

"Yeah, I know. I've been thinking about that. There's really no place to hide. I think you should take him straight to Supernatural Crimes headquarters. Tell Lagatuda what's going on and beg for help. That's all I can think of."

"It'll work. He'll listen. He'll help us," she said, her voice strained with tension.

I winced, hating that I was causing her so much stress. She should be in bed asleep, not getting ready for some insane rescue mission in a stolen truck.

"I'll do my best to hold them off," I said. "And if I get the chance, I'll tell Evan to run like hell to you."

"We'll get him to safety, Ella," she said. "It's going to be okay."

"It'll take a miracle. No matter what, just . . . um—" My voice wavered, and I had to stop. I cleared my throat and tried again. "Just . . . Promise me you'll wear a seat belt."

"I promise." I could hear the faintest of smiles in her voice.

We ended the call, and I pushed Rogan's big coat off me, so I'd be unencumbered when I needed to move. I stuffed the phone in the pocket of my cropped leather jacket. My chain whip, heavy in its pouch on my belt, rattled faintly as I moved, as if a reminder that it was there for my use.

I watched as the activity picked up below, but I didn't dare try to go any closer. Nearly an hour went by, and I started to wonder if this was all just staging for the next day or night. But then the black town cars began to roll in.

Part of me had expected the mages to arrive in some dramatic, otherworldly fashion. They didn't, though. The cars pulled into a neat row, like dark bricks lined up side-by-side. Doors opened, and people began stepping out. Even from such a distance and with only the light of the rip to illuminate the scene, I spotted Damien right away.

My heart skipped a beat. I didn't see Evan anywhere, though. Where were they hiding him?

Keeping low, I moved back over the ridge, so I'd be completely out of sight if anyone happened to look my way. A small flock of minor demons came through the rip, and I caught the mind of one. I kept it flying with the others, waiting for when the flock split up as they usually did. For a few seconds, I was lost in the sensation of flapping wings and cold wind streaming past. Then the flock began to break up, and I turned my demon back in the direction of the rip.

Swooping it low over the surrounding hills, I steered the demon past the news vans and down into the natural depression of the restricted area. More equipment was being unloaded down there, but it didn't look like weaponry.

When my phone buzzed against my ribs, I nearly shrieked. I fumbled to answer it while still keeping control of the demon.

"Hey, the news coverage has started," Deb said. "No live stuff yet, but they're gearing up for it."

"The mages just arrived," I told her. "Damien's there, but I don't see Evan."

"They're playing another fake interview with Evan right now. He's, oh god, he's talking about how he'll go into the rip, and how he knows the risk is great. He said . . . he said he knows he may not make it out of this alive, but that's okay. It's worth the sacrifice."

My anger flared. The mages really were setting up my brother as a martyr, a tragic hero for the ages. A modern sacrifice on the cross for the salvation of humanity.

"It's time," I said. "I'll call if there's anything else I can tell you that might help."

"Okay, we're leaving now."

The call went dead, but I didn't have time to feel anxious about Deb. Another car had just arrived. I watched as I caught another minor demon and sent it in the direction of Lynnette's so I could track the progress of the stolen truck as Deb and the witches made their way here.

My breath hitched as I watched my brother step out of the car that had just pulled up. He stood there with Damien's brother, the one with the death magic who'd yanked me out of the *in-between*. Damien's brother was so close to Evan that their arms touched. They walked unnaturally close to each other toward the Steins and a couple dozen other mages who'd come for the conflux.

The brother must have been controlling Evan somehow, requiring the proximity or maybe even constant contact. Good. If he had to focus on my brother, he wouldn't be able to interfere with me moving between realms.

Spotlights popped on down below. Activity by the news vans picked up and lights went on there, too, as anchors began filming their introductions to the scene. There were a couple dozen vans lined up, and through the eyes of my demon spy, I recognized logos from national news channels. I even recognized the faces of many of the anchors.

The rip pulsed dramatically, as if somehow aware of all the attention focused on the area.

There were no helicopters, and I couldn't see any news people down below. The mages wanted the coverage, but they didn't want any interference. Or maybe Supernatural Forces had ordered media to stay back. Regardless, there were plenty of eyes on the scene, and I suspected that everyone in the U.S.—maybe the world—was tuned into the live feed coming from the area.

My eyes were glued to my brother. Part of me wanted so badly to pop into the *in-between*, ghost down there and rip Evan from the mages' grasp, and race away with him. But Deb and the witches weren't there yet.

I checked in with the progress of the stolen truck. Deb and the others were maybe fifteen minutes away, still. I was antsy, but not too worried. The mages were still milling around. We probably had hours before anything happened.

But just as I started to tell myself the timing would be fine, they started to move toward the rip. Loki whined at my side.

"Easy, boy," I whispered.

Evan was toward the front of the procession of mages. Damien's brother held onto Evan's arm. Damien's parents walked first. And my old partner stood at Evan's other side.

Out of the corner of my eye, I saw more shifting around among the media. They were scrambling. Maybe they hadn't expected any action yet, either.

The mages gathered in a semi-circle about fifty feet from the base of the rip.

Suddenly, I felt and heard a low rumbling vibration under my feet. I swiveled around but then realized it was coming from deep in the earth. The mages were already tapping into the power of the ley lines that ran through the hills.

Oh, shit. They were going to do it *now*.

The mages began to glow as if their skin emitted soft white light. Lightning crackled overhead, arcing down from high above and striking the ground between the mages and the rip. More bolts rained down around them. The air was filling with magic so thick with power I could almost breathe it in.

Damien's brother towed Evan up closer to the rip, left him there, and returned to the other mages. White magic began streaming from the mages and forming a nebulous cloud that crept toward Evan.

I couldn't wait. I faded into the *in-between*. In the realm of souls and mist, I leapt from the ridge and ran. I couldn't see the mages or my brother, but I knew where they were. As I ran, I felt for the ley lines of the *in-between* and drew their silvery power, pulling it until I thought I would explode.

Then, going against the natures of both realms, I materialized back in the land of the living, dragging the *in-between* power with me.

I'd never drawn so much of the death magic. It surged through me, pounding through my living body, punishing me with exquisite pain for trying to force the power to move where it didn't belong.

The mages were ahead of me with their backs turned. They were completely focused on my brother. He was surrounded in a cloud of milky white magic that lifted him off the ground. They were going to shove him up there, into the rip, and hold him there while they streamed magic into him and through him until he died.

Rage spilled through me like a flash flood. I must have screamed because a couple of the mages turned. Damien was one of them. His eyes widened when he saw me.

I felt blood running from my nose, and I smiled grimly as the world went red. Still holding the silver magic of the *in-between*, I drew huge gulping waves of blood magic. I wanted to die, it hurt so much. But the fury within me and my helpless brother in my sights fueled me.

I hurled the crimson magic at the mages. It hit them like a tidal wave, and on contact their skin began to blister and bleed. They shrieked in agony. I took the opening and streamed silver magic at them in bright pulsing bombs. The first I aimed at Sheila. She was clawing at her eyes with bloody nails and didn't even see it coming. The silver blast hit her, and she toppled over and went still. I hadn't destroyed her soul completely, but I'd delivered a serious blow. I hurled more *in-between* magic and more mages collapsed, but I was running down. I couldn't draw much more without blacking out. My nose gushed warm fluid, and my head pounded a hard, agonizing warning. I knew what it meant. I was on the brink. Much more, and there'd be no healing, no coming back.

But they'd released their hold on Evan. He crashed to the dirt in a heap, unmoving. I raced to him and gathered him up in my arms. I didn't have the strength to carry him, though.

"Evan, wake up!" I screamed at his slack face.

Where were Deb and the witches? Close. They were almost there.

I had to try. I had to try to get him out. I slid my arms under his armpits and began stumbling backward, dragging him.

The mages were either still or writhing around in the agony of my blood magic. It wouldn't last, though. I had to hurry. My head swam, and black spots blotched my vision. I had to release my magic, or I'd pass out.

All I could think of was getting Evan away from the Steins. But my legs shook. I could barely stand.

There were shouts. Soldiers running. At first I thought they were coming for me. But they were looking past me. Then I felt the magic flare from the rip. Something huge flew overhead, low enough to stir up wind with its wings. An arch-demon. I looked up. Two more of them came through the rip.

I stumbled. Movement on the ground drew my eyes. The blood magic was dissipating. The mages were getting to their feet. Damien had me in his sights.

"No," I breathed. "No, you can't have him."

My former partner and friend walked toward me, and as I watched him move, it was as if the world had slowed down. I tried to keep going, but I was too weak.

"He's ours, Ella," Damien said. But it wasn't Damien. My friend was gone. "Just give him to us, and it'll be over soon."

"No," I tried to shout, but it came out more of a grunt.

Damien reached for Evan's arm. I managed to draw a bit of fire magic and spray it like a blow torch at Damien's face. I felt a sharp snap in each temple and blood started to leak from my ears. He jumped back and ducked, and the red magic blew past him and went out.

I let my brother fall and stepped in between him and Damien. Lightning quick, my whip was in my hand and imbued with elemental magic. I could only pull weak strands of earth and fire, but I stubbornly flicked the razor chain at Damien.

He gave me a look that was almost kind, except for the coldness in his mage eyes, with the galaxies glowing in his pupils.

"Don't do this," I said. There was nothing else to do but beg. I was bleeding to death, and I couldn't pull more power. "Evan is innocent. He didn't choose this. This is murder."

"It's a sacrifice," Damien said. "A worthy one."

"Bullshit," I spat. Arch-demons were streaming through the rip overhead, but I ignored the commotion of the creatures and the soldiers as they scrambled to control the situation.

Damien's father called out to him, but Damien raised a hand, holding him off.

"You're better than this. You're better than them," I said, gesturing at the mages. "You're not a cold-blooded killer. You're intelligent and curious and *kind*. You've known love. That man in your pictures, the one who helped you in San Francisco. He made you happy, and you did the same for him. I'd bet anything that you felt completely whole in those happy moments. You don't need anyone's approval, Damien. You've known freedom from all that Order nonsense, from your family's judgment. That was a gift, and you never even knew it."

I was babbling, trying to stall. My head still felt like it might explode, but the pounding had subsided. I had one last burst of magic in me. I just had to wait until Deb and the witches could get close enough to take Evan away. They'd reached the site and were trying to weave through the chaos. They'd gotten stalled somewhere behind me, but I couldn't turn to look, and I'd lost control of my spies.

But the mages had recovered. Even Sheila was on her feet again. White magic surrounded them, and they had their sights on me. I swung my arm and my whip arced out. It caught Damien on the chin, so fast he didn't even feel it coming. He touched it, and his fingers came away bloody.

I whirled the whip overhead, hollering like a madwoman and swinging the razor chain at the mages. I must have looked crazy enough to give them pause because they stopped their advance. But the reprieve only lasted a few seconds. Then they were drawing magic and closing in.

Tossing one last desperate look at Damien, I froze for a split second because I could have sworn his eyes had filled with tears. The chill and condescension that had made his face so unbearably placid seemed to have broken. Maybe I'd gotten through? But he wasn't moving to help. I couldn't wait.

I charged. It was my last resort. When I breached the glow of the white mage magic, agony ripped through me. Every muscle went rigid. My whip fell from my hand, and I collapsed.

I truly believed I'd failed. But there was a sound, far away at first. A low, powerful, primal sound that cut through everything else.

It was the howl of a hellhound.

A black form blurred past. Loki. Then another. I thought I was seeing double. But no, there was a whole pack of hellhounds. They were leaping out of the lower edge of the rip and following my dog. In a hurricane of gnashing teeth and hellfire eyes, they raced around me and the mages with barks that seemed to originate from hell itself.

Something tickled at my memory. When the Manhattan Rip first tore into the world, hellhounds had poured through.

They'd herded victims for their demons, causing destruction and chaos until they were captured and destroyed.

But not all of them. Some had escaped, and that was how my Loki had come to be.

The pain lessened as I watched my dog lead his pack as they lunged and bit at the mages. The Steins and their Order turned their powers on the hellhounds, but the dogs were either impervious to the magic or didn't feel it in their frenzy. They kept running, forcing the mages into a tighter bunch. Overhead, arch-demons circled.

I wanted desperately to scramble out of the way, because I knew what was coming. The hellhounds were gathering victims for the arch-demons, and the great winged creatures would dive, transform, and stream into the eyes to take possession.

But Damien, Evan, and I had been excluded from the round-up. No longer pummeled by mage magic, I struggled to stand. Failing that, I crawled to my brother while Damien tried to help the mages by fighting off the hellhounds.

Behind me, wheels skidded on the dry packed dirt of the desert, and I whipped around. Deb had made it through. A door popped open on the truck, and witches from my coven spilled out, gathered my brother up, and shoved him inside. The vehicle was surrounded with gyrating lines of magic, a tightly-woven shield of magic. Not only did it have the protection of the witches' power, it was armored against magical attacks and demons. Once the doors were shut, even Damien couldn't penetrate the truck.

Just as they started to come back for me, the agony of a mage magic onslaught returned.

"Go! Go now!" I screamed. Then I lost consciousness.

When I awoke, I was bathed in a white glow and suspended in the air. For a second, I thought I was dead. That guess actually wasn't so far off.

In my periphery, beyond the white magic that seemed to compress the air against me, there were licks of neon blue. I'd been raised into the air and centered in the rip. But something was off. I was wearing . . . Evan's clothes?

Feeling foggy, slow, and not as concerned as I knew I should be, I tipped my gaze downward. My body seemed frozen, but I could move my head. Seeing Loki in his hellhound form below, still herding the mages as arch-demons swooped in to attempt possession one-by-one, sobered me up fast.

It looked like I was wearing Evan's clothes, but I could feel the illusion magic clinging to me. My heart sank. The mages had used magic to make me look like Evan. To everyone below, everyone watching on TV, it appeared the young man who had volunteered to try to close the rips was doing just that.

The mages had formed a shield that was doing a decent job of protecting them against the diving arch-demons. The creatures screamed in frustration as they tried to get at their prey. Blasts from the Supernatural Forces guns lit up the sky as the soldiers tried to battle the huge ripspawn. It was a fricking miracle one of the blasts hadn't already hit me.

Damien still stood outside the ring of hellhounds. Maybe Loki didn't realize that Damien was no longer our friend. I couldn't really fault the pooch. I'd thought that Damien was the one holding me suspended in the air, but he wasn't. Sheila Stein stood in the midst of the dogs and the swooping hellspawn, calm as if she was skygazing on a summer day. The white magic flowed in a split river, one stream leading up to me and the other to Damien.

Then I understood that Damien wasn't just a spectator. He was frozen in place, only his blue eyes able to swivel around in his head. Sheila was holding him hostage with her magic, too.

My heart thumped in panic as I swung my eyes to the spot where I'd left Evan. He was gone. So was the stolen armored truck. They'd gotten away or gotten detained somewhere. It didn't matter because Evan wasn't up here. That meant he'd escaped the mages. I had no idea how Deb and the witches had managed it, but somehow, they'd gotten him out.

Tears of relief flooded my eyes, mingling with the blood that was crusted under my nose and across my cheeks. Evan had escaped.

Sheila and the mages must have thought that I, being Evan's biological sister, was a suitable replacement for the magical conduit that would seal the interdimensional tears forever. I was willing to let her think so until the very last moment, in order to give Deb and the others more time to get to Lagatuda at Supernatural Crimes and get amnesty for Evan.

When I saw some of the other mages below had begun to draw their pure white power, I knew I needed to make my exit before it was too late. I turned inward, to the reaper who resided within me, ready to let his nature take over and carry us to the safety of limbo land.

I waited for the shift to the *in-between*. Instead of fading into the gray mist, my head rang like a gong. It was a horrible vibrating pain and pressure that made me want to claw my eyes out just to try to relieve the growing torture inside my head.

Shuddering and taking heaving breaths, I opened my eyes. I was still in the realm of the living.

I tried again. And failed.

Damien's brother, standing next to Sheila, smiled up at me. I didn't even know that bastard's name, but he was down there gloating as he blocked me from the *in-between*.

A new realization hit. I wasn't getting away. The *in-between* had been my escape route, but I could no longer use it. I blinked, trying to absorb the idea of my own death.

Panic began to rise up as I desperately looked for something, anything, that could save me. I could somehow feel that the illusion magic was even distorting my expression, probably making it appear that I was concentrating, hard at work with my own magic in my effort to save humanity.

I wasn't getting away. I was going to die.

Seeking comfort, my gaze automatically went to Damien. His was the only familiar face below, the only one who had ever been warm or friendly. But there was no comfort there.

I closed my eyes. "Evan is safe," I whispered to myself.

Then I looked down at my former partner again.

"My mother thinks you'll be enough," he said, somehow projecting his voice so I could hear through the din of demons, blasts, and magic. His voice was strained, his words halting. "She thinks they can use you to close the rips, even though I told them it would be imperfect. Likely much worse. She refuses to listen. She won't let you go, and no one will stand up to her even if they think I'm right."

I could tell he was in immense pain by the way he was grinding out the words. He was trying to push back against the magical restraint.

"It's okay, Damien," I said. I spoke the words softly, but I could tell he'd heard. I could see it in his face. I wasn't even sure why, but for some reason I wanted Damien to know that I could forgive him as long as my brother didn't die. "Better me than Evan."

"I'm sorry Ella," he said. The magic that held me began to pierce into me like spikes. The pain began to consume my attention, but I forced my eyelids to remain open. I wasn't sure if I was still hearing his words or only reading his lips, but I was positive of what he was saying.

He began shaking his head, and his chin trembled. "I'm so sorry for everything. So sorry, so sorry."

He kept repeating the phrase, but I could barely see him. The mages were powering up, and the magic around me was growing uncomfortably hot. It was also becoming unbearably bright. My skin began to burn. I had to close my eyes. The fire of the magic seared my lungs. I tried to hold my breath.

It was so hot I prayed I'd lose consciousness. But the seconds ticked by, and it only got worse. My burning lips parted, and my moans turned into agonized screams.

Then something slammed into me and I was tumbling. In the split second before I landed, I recognized the signature of the magic that had broken me free of the mages' hold. It was Damien's. He'd somehow overpowered the others.

I thought I heard his voice whisper through my mind, saying, "I'm not the perfect solution either, but maybe that's not what the world needs."

I hit the ground hard, my hip, shoulder, and temple slamming the dirt.

I had a perfect view of Damien as he hung suspended in the air like a superhero. He burned up in the white-hot magic a split second before the rip shrank down to nothing, swallowing Damien, and the neon blue flames winked out.

Five months later

I woke up to something wet running across my neck and an unpleasant smell filling my nose. I grinned, though. I couldn't help it.

"Somebody did a doody," I cooed in a high-pitched voice and adjusted the warm bundle in my arms.

I'd dozed off with Gretchen on my chest. Her face had been tucked against my neck, and she'd drooled.

Deb's giggle drew my attention to the stairs leading up to the second floor. "Did you seriously just say *doody* and smile?" she asked.

My grin turned sheepish. "Nah, you must have heard wrong."

I managed to maneuver out of the easy chair and to a standing position without using my hands.

Deb came to me with her arms outstretched. "Here, I'll change her."

Before Deb could claim her newborn daughter, big hands swooped in from the side.

"Nope! Denied," Evan crowed as he whisked Gretchen away from me and toward the first-floor office where a changing table was set up.

I could hear him singing to her, and she started burbling back. My smile broadened at the sound of my brother's voice—lucid and strong. I would never get tired of it. One unexpected benefit of his captivity with Damien was that my brother had gotten clean. He'd done well since the conflux, attending addict support groups and doing outpatient counseling, but I knew there would be ups and downs. He was still fragile in many ways.

"I swear they have their own secret language," Deb said.

I laughed. "I can't believe my brother loves babies so much."

I kept expecting the novelty of hanging out at home and helping with Gretchen to wear off, for Evan to start dating or get interested in music or video games or any one of the number of normal things he'd missed out on. But he adored Gretchen—the feeding, the diapers, the tiny clothes, all of it. It seemed to do him good to focus on caring for someone else. When he wasn't hanging out with the baby, he was exploring his magic. The charm my mother had put in place so long ago to conceal his unique powers had been removed by the mages right before the conflux. Evan didn't have strange magics like I did, but in addition to being a natural low Level III, he could do crazy things with his power, like make the strands of magic invisible to other crafters. Distance seemed to be no barrier for him, and he could cast his magic remotely to places that were miles away, as long as he could adequately visualize the location. He was working with a mentor Deb had found, and it seemed every week he was discovering some new trick.

Evan's mentor was one of the few people we'd met since the conflux. We didn't have much to do with anyone outside our immediate circle. My name had been cleared and all accusations dropped, but there was still a lot of media fallout over the conflux, what the press called the Cataclysm. I had no desire to follow any of the coverage. The media had called for my head once, and it had soured me forever. I'd only watched one report since the Cataclysm, the one that aired when news of my uncle Jacob Gregori's arrest broke. Apparently, Phillip Zarella's information had been good. Jacob would most likely spend the rest of his life in prison. Zarella seemed to have disappeared, but I didn't expect him to stay in hiding forever.

Insulated as we tried to be, we couldn't completely ignore the effects of the Cataclysm. By some miracle, Damien's sacrifice had closed the rips. But because he wasn't Evan, there had been some side effects. The Cataclysm had sent shockwaves through the magical world and changed magic in ways that weren't fully understood yet. I felt the shift every time I drew power. The elements were intermingled now. Level Is and some lower Level IIs were no longer able to draw only a single magical element—if they pulled magic, they pulled some of everything. Powerful crafters could separate the elements with some concerted effort, but those without enough power to do this basically had to relearn magic. I hadn't spent much time playing around with it. I didn't have a lot of need to sling magic since the Cataclysm, and I didn't really want to. For one, it was safer if I didn't. I had damage that no healer could undo, and using magic was painful and affected my short-term memory. And, the changes in the ways magic worked were still too sharp a reminder of Damien's death.

In the time since the Cataclysm, I'd gone through the full range of grief emotions, much as I'd tried to resist it. I used to have flashes of anger at Damien. But I'd realized I wasn't truly angry—just grieving. Those had mostly subsided, and in their place was a poignant, sorrowful loving gratitude that made my chest ache every time it snuck up on me.

I was content to sink into the company of the people I loved. Deb and I had found a much larger house to rent, which was made possible after I sold the rights to my official biography. Deb and I had discussed moving into Rogan's house, but it only had two bedrooms and one bath and so wasn't much better than my old place. Plus, I didn't want the constant reminder of his death. The book advance I received was more money than I'd ever imagined, even after my agent took her cut. I never would have pursued a book deal at all, if not for the need to provide a home and treatment for Evan and the desire to help ease things for Deb. I got the payout before Deb's new coven charter went through—yep, she was a Moon Priestess and I'd decided to join her—so I wasn't obligated to put it into the organization's coffers, but I made a big donation to the coven's account to get us started.

I could have bought a house, but we'd decided on renting instead because we'd all had the sense that our current arrangement could be fleeting.

Chris Lagatuda had started hanging around more and more after the Cataclysm—even my notoriety wasn't enough to drive him away from Deb, it seemed—and the two of them made googly eyes at each other over Gretchen pretty much constantly.

As it turned out, we were right about impending changes. A week prior, Chris had asked me to meet him downtown alone, which had seemed incredibly odd until he took me to a jewelry store to show me a diamond ring and ask me if I thought Deb would like it. He'd also asked for my blessing as a stand-in for Deb's parents, who she'd never known. I'd wiped away a tear as I'd given it, and Chris got a little choked up, too.

I heard the front door open, and a moment later the tall detective appeared in the living room.

"Speak of the devil," I said.

"Hey, Ella, how are you?" Chris asked. He was already looking around for the baby. Gretchen had more admirers than she knew what to do with.

"Pretty good. Evan's got the kid," I said. I gave him a conspiratorial look and lowered my voice to a whisper. "Everything's all set."

He nodded just as Deb reappeared, her face breaking into a sunny smile at the sight of Chris.

"I didn't know you were coming over," she said, obviously delighted by the surprise.

She went to him and practically had to jump to throw her arms around his neck. They kissed for so long I finally had to clear my throat.

Chris gave me a sheepish look.

"The witches are going to start arriving any second," Deb said to Chris. "But we could get together after?"

"Sure, I just wanted to say hi," he said. "I'll get out of your way."

He kissed her forehead just as my phone vibrated. I glanced at the message. *We're ready.*

My eyes met Chris's, and I gave him a tiny nod.

Evan had come out with Gretchen. He was in charge of keeping Deb in the house for a couple of minutes while we got into position in the back yard.

I headed toward the back door that led to the yard while Chris scooted out the front door.

"Ella?" Deb's voice trailed after me.

I gave her a little wave but didn't respond. She'd see soon enough what was up.

In the perfectly square swath of lawn that had finally fully greened up in the past couple of weeks as May had dissipated the last chill of winter, the witches of the new coven had gathered. Eleven women stood in a circle holding little bunches of spring flowers.

Roxanne waited outside the back door with a huge smile on her face. She handed me my own bouquet, and I squeezed her arm and gave her a big grin.

I went and stood in the space that had been made for me, in between Becky and Adriana, in the circle of witches. The sun had set, and the sky was streaked with orange-pink on the western horizon. It wasn't summer yet, but the evening was warmer than usual, and the air carried the decidedly summery scent of cut grass.

Chris came through the side gate and jogged into the middle of the circle. He was panting a little harder than the short walk around the house warranted, obviously nervous.

Roxanne was still at the back door, watching for Deb. The young witch straightened and raised her hand at us. She was technically too young to be in a coven—the minimum age was sixteen—but Deb had applied to the governing body of the covens for an exception, and it had been granted. Jen was part of the new coven, too. She'd confessed that Lynnette had drawn her in with her charm. Then the former coven lead had started her manipulations, making subtle threats about exposing Jen's unique powers to people who would try to take advantage of her. I was glad to have Jen back.

Together, the other witches and I drew magic. Using the elements in purely decorative ways, some of the women wove strands in a series of arches that led from the back door to our circle. I pulled blue air and red fire, concentrating hard on separating the single elements from the others that tried to join them, and made little dots of it wink on and off like fireflies. It only caused a little pain behind my eyes.

When Roxanne opened the door and Deb stepped out, she stopped short and her jaw dropped. She caught sight of Chris in the circle and pressed her lips together. Her expression was trembling, balancing on the edge between tears and laughter.

Roxanne took Deb's hand, leading her away from the house and through the arches we'd created. Evan walked behind them with Gretchen in his arms. Loki brought up the rear of the procession, trotting along behind my brother like there was no question a hellhound-labradoodle had a place in the little ceremony.

At the edge of the circle, Roxanne stopped and gently nudged Deb to go ahead. Just as she stepped inside the circle, Chris got down on one knee. She didn't even make it two steps before tears were streaming down her pink cheeks. She was smiling so hard, her blue eyes were nearly pinched shut.

He presented the ring he'd shown me and spoke quiet words to her, and I only half listened as I watched the couple and basked in the pure delight and affection that welled up between them.

Chris slipped the ring onto her finger, stood, and pulled her into his arms. Their lips met, and that was our cue. In the fading light of evening, I and the other witches made a brief little magical fireworks show above the newly-engaged couple. By the time the last spark died out, there wasn't a dry eye in the yard.

After a round of hugs and congratulations, we all trooped back inside. The others gathered in the living room while Roxanne and I went into the kitchen. I'd almost forgone the champagne because that had been Lynnette's thing. But Deb loved a glass of bubbly, so I'd bought three bottles of the expensive stuff. Roxanne had made a congratulations cake, and some of the other women had brought various goodies.

Just as I filled the last plastic disposable flute—it wasn't my style to own a full set of champagne glasses—my phone vibrated. A message from Caleb Montgomery. I paused to read it.

Don't judge me, but I want to hear every detail of the proposal. Like, every. Single. Thing.

I bit my lower lip, hiding a smile as I typed a reply: *Aw, you're such a romantic. It was amazing.*

Can you come over tonight after I'm off shift?

I smiled in earnest, unable to hold it back.

I'll be at your place at ten.

Miracle of miracles, Caleb had actually still wanted to date me. He'd tried to contact me even before my name was cleared, but I'd been extremely difficult to get a hold of for a while, and he hadn't known how to reach me. Even after the Cataclysm, I'd told him I wasn't ready for a serious relationship. He'd waited a month and asked again. I'd said no. He waited another month. I said no again and didn't expect he'd risk another rejection. But he had, and I finally said yes.

I carried the tray of plastic champagne flutes out into the living room, with Roxanne trailing behind me holding the cake. We toasted Deb and Chris. Then one of the new witches in the coven, Toshiko, stepped forward.

"I know we're here to celebrate the engagement, and I don't want to take anything away from that," she said. "But I also just want to say how happy I am to be part of this group, this family of witches. I know this coven experienced a lot of pain to get to this point. That's not lost on me or any of the other new girls. But it's my great fortune—*our* great fortune—that it allowed me to join you. And I can't imagine pledging my loyalty to any other Moon Priestess."

With that, she turned to Deb. Toshiko raised her glass and the rest of us did, too, toasting Deb, our leader. Our new charter had only been official for a few weeks, but it was as if Deb had always led her own coven, as if she'd been born to do it.

We no longer worried about Lynnette trying to get anything from us. After the Cataclysm, both federal and supernatural charges had been leveled against her. She'd fled, and rumor was she'd changed her name and appearance. Before she'd disappeared, I'd let her know that if she ever tried to contact any of the coven witches or interfere in our lives or coven business in any way, I'd end her. I wasn't a killer, but I was powerful enough to follow up on the threat and she knew it. Elena and Marta had apparently also left the area. Deb had been right about Jen, though, and we'd reconciled with her. She'd remained a part of the coven, though she was forbidden from accessing any of the organization's records or accounts.

Chris stuck around for cake and then made his exit. Evan went upstairs with the baby, leaving us women alone in the living room.

We never got around to any coven business. There would always be another meeting for that.

By the time the women began to trickle out and head home, it was past nine and Deb was yawning. Evan and I were on a rotation with Deb, taking turns helping out with

Gretchen at night, but Deb still had to get up to pump breastmilk every night, whereas I at least got a full night's sleep two out of three days.

Roxanne had already gone to her room and was probably lying in bed watching videos on her phone.

Deb stood, stretched, and yawned again, so wide her jaw cracked. She looked down at the sparkling diamond on her finger.

"Do you think it's too soon?" she asked.

"What's too soon?"

"Are Chris and I doing this too fast?"

I scoffed. "Nah, I think you're doing it perfectly."

She smiled, her blue eyes sparkling. "Thank you for everything."

I waved a hand. "You don't have to thank me." I seriously did not want to cry yet again that night.

She rushed me and threw her arms around my neck in a fierce hug. "You will always be my family, Ella."

I pulled my lips in between my teeth and bit down hard as I returned her embrace.

"Congratulations," I said. "You deserve everything you desire."

She pulled back and laughed, a dreamy look in her blue eyes. "I think I actually *have* everything I desire. How crazy is that?"

I made shooing motions at her. "Get to bed while you can."

I poked my head into Evan's room, to let him know I was leaving for the night, and then called Loki. After the night of the conflux, we were even more inseparable than before. It was just understood that we were a package deal. Fortunately, Caleb seemed to love the hellhound-doodle. In the garage, Loki jumped into the bed of my old truck.

As I drove away from the house, my eyes were drawn to the northwest, where the Boise Rip had been. An ache still clutched at my heart every time I thought of it, because with it came the image of Damien disappearing into the neon blue flames of magic. But I tried to remind myself that he'd made his choice freely, that he'd finally found redemption and, I hoped, peace. Maybe someday the memories would hurt less.

I drew a deep breath and pulled myself into the present, to the glow of the evening's happiness that still surrounded me, and to the anticipation of happy days and celebrations ahead. I had more good things going for me than I'd ever dared imagine. My reaper and I had found peace. I had my brother back. A good man in my life. And I had Deb, Gretchen, Roxanne, and the coven. They were all the family I needed.

About the Author

Jayne Faith writes fantasy set in the real world. She's a meditator, dog lover, TV addict, clean eater, homebody, sun baby, and Sagittarius. Her superpower is her laugh. She owns way too many colored pens and pairs of jeans. Visit her website at www.jaynefaith.com, where you can sign up for her VIP list and get free books.

www.ingramcontent.com/pod-product-compliance
Lightning Source LLC
Chambersburg PA
CBHW031554240626
47153CB00002B/496